OutRageous

SHEILA ORTIZ-TAYLOR

Spinsters Ink

2006

Spinsters Ink, Inc.
P.O. Box 242
Midway, FL 32343

Printed in the United States of America on acid-free paper
First Edition

Editor: Anna Chinappi
Cover designer: LA Callaghan

ISBN 1-883523-72-9

For Barbara Grier and Donna McBride

Acknowledgments

I would like to thank Andrea Otañez and Joy Lynn Lewis for reading drafts of this manuscript; Christina Strobel for helping me to understand Arden's philosophy, Joann Gardner, her pedagogy, Sandra Ortiz Taylor, her cosmology, Cadence Kidwell, her horticulture and Joyce B. Lewis, Bertha Michael's subtle appreciation of fine china cups.

Many institutions helped me shape and complete this novel. I am particularly grateful to the Florida Arts Council for an Individual Artist Fellowship, to the Dorland Mountain Arts Colony and the Hambidge Center for writers' residencies and to the English Department at Florida State University for financial and moral support.

Earlier versions of several chapters first appeared in *U.S. Latino Literatures and Cultures: Transnational Perspectives*, Francisco A. Lomelí and Karin Ikas, eds. (Heidelberg: Universitälsverlag C. Winter, 2000) pp. 283-293, and in *Double Crossings*, Mario Martín Flores and Carlos von Son, eds. (New Jersey: Ediciones Nuevo Espacio: Colección Academia, 2001), pp. 225-238.

About the Author

Sheila Ortiz Taylor has taught fiction writing and literature at Florida State University for more than thirty years. Her first novel, *Faultline* (Naiad Press 1982), is part of a Chicana lesbian trilogy that includes *Southbound* and the present volume, *OutRageous*. Other works include the novels *Spring Forward/Fall Back* and *Coachella*, as well as a volume of poetry, *Slow Dancing at Miss Polly's*, and the family memoir, *Imaginary Parents*. She lives in Florida with her partner of fifteen years.

Chapter 1

Go Ask Alice

A hearse as blue as a north Florida sky purred toward Tallahassee, sun glinting off roof and hood. Out the driver side window a woman's small hand gestured to the lyrics of Grace Slick: "One pill makes you larger, and one pill makes you small." Along the passenger side window a brown arm lounged, fingers tapping accompaniment to the line, "But the one your mother gives you, doesn't do a thing at all."

Arden Benbow, unlikely refugee from southern California and equally unlikely new assistant professor of English at Midway College, approached employment and the American South with a naïveté that made falling down a rabbit hole or for that matter passing through the looking glass seem like child's play. Her friend Topaz Wilson had come along to protect her from he knew not what. Perhaps from Southern culture, perhaps from her own fecund imagination. He leaned forward and snapped off the radio.

But he could not hear much less control the sounds in her head, the continuing interior monologue describing the new and surprising trajectory of her own sweet life. In the middle of this delicious April in 1973, she had a real job in a new place. Life, which she tended to think of as a complex novel, or—after the great Henry Fielding—"a comic epic poem in prose," life itself now set before her a fresh chapter, a chapter whose opening letters were decorated in all the gay colors of an antique manuscript.

CHAPTER, THE FIRST, IN WHICH ARDEN BENBOW, OUR POET HERO, ENTERS THE JEWELED CITY.

And the prospect did promise jewels. Along either side of the highway, waist-high grass of an improbable green defined each curve, a green she had never known in the seared southern California rolling hills she had always adored, in the land of her mother and her mother's mother and her mother's mother's mother. She perhaps felt, despite her *Californio* lineage, her devotion begin to waver, to wander toward this new, lovely one, she who shimmered in moist heat and seductive promise: *La Florida*.

Arden drummed her hands on the steering wheel and looked out at voluptuous grasslands that seemed to part before the Cadillac's hood ornament like a healthy head of green hair through which she was driving.

She had always thought of states by color. Colorado, of course, was paprika. Washington was slate blue. Idaho, baked potato brown. Maine, cerulean. Florida, on her personal color chart, had always been yellow, but she saw now she had been mistaken, that it was instead rolling shades of yellow-tinged, blue-rooted, purple-tipped green. Had she not all her life been hungry for green, starved for it, like a lost sailor scarcely surviving on a diet of the driest hardtack?

She vowed to drop anchor here, right here in this green field, and live forever. Florida, La Guapa, the handsome woman to whom—at this very minute—she must somehow award the passion flower of her heart. Florida.

She felt faintly adulterous, thought guiltily of her lover Alice, at this moment three thousand miles away caring for the six children that Arden herself had given birth to, heard in her mind Alice say, "Oh

Arden, you are so Catholic," and so dismissed the pang, allowed herself the innocence of falling in love with a state, a geography, a demography. The simple innocence of it.

And what was innocence, anyway? What, passion?

"She's heating up again," said Topaz, leaning in toward the wheel to read through dazzling glare the gauge on the dash. "Better pull over and let her breathe a while."

"Let's stop for lunch, then. Florida makes me hungry. It looks like a salad."

"What do people eat here anyway," asked Topaz in a mistrustful tone, "in this Florida?"

"Didn't we have wonderful food in Louisiana?" said Arden in dreamy recollection.

"That was then. Goodbye Louisiana, hello Florida."

"Pessimist. I'm going to find us some fine native food. We'll eat whatever it is Floridians eat."

"Chain cuisine. You know that. You can feel it."

"There," said Arden, pointing across her companion at a sign already vanishing. "'Eat at Glenda's!' it says. That's no chain. Glenda herself is preparing our lunch right now. She rose before daylight. I hear her scrubbing the carrots."

"I don't like to eat at places that tell me to eat there. It sets up a positive resistance. *Eat here.* The gastronomical imperative, a mood that takes my appetite clean away."

"Nothing takes your appetite away. Besides, you said yourself the engine's overheating."

Topaz turned to make sure the U-Haul was dutifully following the laboring hearse. "I hate that trailer," he said. "I wish the damn thing had fallen into that ravine back in Texas."

"No you don't. And here's Glenda's." She slowed down. "Look, trucks. Four semis and a pickup."

"What makes people think truck drivers know where to eat? We don't copy anything else they do. We don't like the way they vote. We don't even like the way they drive."

Arden turned into the gravel parking lot and pulled up next to a glittering black Peterbilt that said in red letters, "Grandma's Kuntry Cookin'."

"I hate to say I told you so."

"You *love* to say I told you so."

He laughed in admission, slung his pith helmet into the back seat and emerged into the heat of early June, whereupon his sunglasses immediately fogged up. He stretched out to his customary six-foot-three length and called to his friend, who was checking the trailer hitch. "I'm blind, Arden. Just like Bette Davis in *Dark Victory* before she staggered into the garden and died nobly."

"It wasn't the garden," Arden said gently, taking off his shades and slipping them into her breast pocket. "She died at the foot of the spiral staircase."

"I like that even better," said Topaz taking her arm.

They crunched across glittering rock toward the entrance. The dim, frigid interior smelled like Gravy Master. A large, handmade sign advised, "Faith should be your steering wheel not your spare tire. Wait here for hostess." Four truck drivers in separate booths and three teenage girls in another all stared at them, suspending time.

The long silence eventually had its effect. Glenda herself emerged through swinging doors, wiping her hands down the front of an apron decorated with the culinary history of the day. She stopped dead and took in the two strangers. "You two together then?" Glenda fumbled for laminated menus. Then she led them in the direction of an empty dining room where rows of tables seemed to slumber in the half-light.

Arden came to a sudden halt and said, "We'd rather be in there with the other truck drivers. We're not much on formality."

"Y'all truck drivers then, sure 'nough?" Glenda squinted out the weeping, sun-drenched plate glass into the parking lot, searching for clues to their identity.

"In a manner of speaking," Arden said.

"Transportin' a corpse, looks to me like. Land sakes. Haven't seen a hearse like that in twenty years. Chillin' sight. Two of you musta worked up an appetite, though."

Topaz eyed the sign that said, "If our waitresses start to act grumpy,

please notify management and we'll administer additional medica-
tion."

"I wrote that," said Glenda, with pride of authorship. "This here's
my place." She stood motionless, having lost the thread of her narration.

"Glenda," said Arden, "it was your charming sign out on the highway that accounts for these strangers on your doorstep. Do you suppose
we could see a little of that Southern hospitality which so obviously has
inspired this charming and unique enterprise of yours?"

"Oh yes ma'am," said Glenda, recovering her manners. "Now y'all
just sit yourselves down right here by the window, and I'll bring you
some nice cold tea." She set the menus down next to cutlery rolled tight
in paper napkins like tiny hostages.

When she was out of sight, Arden said, "Nobody ever called me that
before."

"Called you what?" asked Topaz, studying the menu. "And what's
that tone?"

"Ma'am. She called me ma'am."

Topaz dropped his menu. "You've been called a lot of things in your
time to be complaining about a little ma'am-ing? The real issue here is
the honest-to-God fried bologna sandwich on this menu. And what's a
corn dog, anyway?"

"What if she called you sir?"

"Not in this lifetime she wouldn't. Culture forbids it. No, Glenda's
got another word she's keeping for me. I know about the South." He
reached across the table for his sunglasses.

"You know about *movies* about the South," she said, handing them
over.

"Art imitates life." He put on his glasses and through dark lenses
watched Glenda approach with their tea.

"Can I bring y'all the special?" Glenda asked, clunking down per-
spiring red plastic tumblers before the travelers.

"Yes," said Arden, recovering her humor, "we'll both have the special."

"Actually I was interested in your fried bologna sandwich."

"Gone as yesterday. Same for the mullet basket. But I can get you the special if you want, like your . . . friend here is having. Folks around here seem to like it just fine."

Topaz nodded, surrendered his menu, and Glenda drifted off toward the kitchen in big, dingy nurse shoes. As soon as she disappeared through the double doors, he sank his head into his hands. "Not the special. I could have had a corn dog. Whatever that is."

"Today, Topaz, we're going to eat what Floridians eat. The special."

"We're going to eat what truck drivers eat. Did you see that display up by the cash register? Right there under the sign that says, 'Buckle up for Jesus'? They've got the whole Trinity up there: Alka Seltzer, Tums and Pepto-Bismol. Truck drivers live on stomach remedies."

Topaz unrolled his napkin, sending knife and fork skittering across the table. In the silence that followed, his eye fell on a truck driver in a faded red cap, holding his barbecued pork sandwich in two enormous hands as if the bun were the steering wheel of his truck. The man fixed him in the crosshairs of his undivided attention.

"Oh shit," said Topaz, "I was afraid of this. He thinks you're a white woman—or should I say lady—and he *knows* I'm a black man, and he assumes that everybody here is heterosexual, despite compelling evidence to the contrary. Now he's wondering exactly where his responsibilities lie."

Just then Glenda burst through double doors with a heavy plate on each hand, caught the gaze of the truck driver and gave her beehive an almost imperceptible shake, transmitting the ancient coded warning from Southern female to Southern male that meant: *Now you behave yourself, hear?* Bubba swallowed the last bite, reached for his check and heaved himself up onto his Red Wings.

Glenda set down the heavy plates and avoiding eye contact, observed, "Don't guess you folks are from anywhere around here. You look like you came from a *long* ways off."

Topaz regarded his plate, which resembled an aerial photograph of an Arabian desert.

"We're from California," said Arden, lifting her fork.

At the word, "California," *everyone* looked—the man in the red hat waiting at the cash register, the other truckers, the teenagers and a middle-aged black man who came out of the kitchen wearing an apron streaked with colors that matched up with the aerial photographs of the Arabian desert.

"But I'm moving to Tallahassee. Well, actually to Midway," Arden corrected herself. "I guess it's practically the same thing."

"Not hardly," said Glenda, fixing her eyes on Topaz, who was directing his fork into the side of a perfect volcano of mashed potatoes, thereby releasing a torrent of brown gravy onto his fried okra, field peas and summer squash.

"My compliments to the chef," he murmured.

"And you're not?" Glenda asked him.

"Not what?"

"Not moving to Midway."

"My dear lady, not for all the sweet tea in Florida."

"That's a no?"

"That's an unequivocal no."

"*I* live in Midway," said Glenda, looking now into Arden's eyes, her expression easing. "Welcome stranger."

"Is there a motel in Midway you can recommend?" Arden asked, sawing with her dull knife through layers of leathery roast beef suspended on a bed of spongy white bread.

"There's not no motel at all," Glenda said. "Only a IGA grocery and the Unocal gas station. Throw in the food stamp store, the Baptist church and Ace Hardware and you've just about got Midway. Oh, and the college, of course. But they keep to theyselves, that bunch. For a hotel, though, you'll have to go on in to Tallahassee. It ain't that far. Twenty minutes, maybe. I'll leave y'all to enjoy your dinner now. Need anything else, just give us a holler."

Topaz sipped his drink and grimaced. "I hate sugary iced tea, and I hate Florida even worse."

Arden thoughtfully crunched up fried medallions of okra. "It was you who said I should take this job in the first place. You said Florida was not the South, Florida was just Florida. Oranges and Cubans and Disney World. You liked the money, too, as I recall."

"That's true. You do need money. Six kids is a lot of kids to have. Okay, keep the job then, Arden. But just be careful, for Christ's sake. Bust your cards, as my Aunt Hazel used to say. Southerners can play rough, and some of them can play subtle." He lifted a flap of meat and looked under it suspiciously.

"Topaz, my way is to march forward, assuming the best."

"Until your ass gets whipped."

"My ass has never been whipped in *your* memory."

"Just be careful is all I'm saying. Marching straight ahead holding your damn musket in front of you and the flag over your head may not get it anymore, Arden. You got to take the clue from your ancestors and start hiding behind rocks and planning your own little surprises for the damned enemy."

"I have heard you, o wise one."

"Just eat your peas and let's get the hell on out of here."

"At least I know how to watch my language in public, while a guest of the South."

"What language?"

"You just said Christ, hell and damn in as many seconds," she remarked, laying her knife and fork across her plate. "We Southern ladies don't tolerate language like that." She rolled her eyes demurely in the direction of a placard over the cash register that read, "I'm an organ donor. I gave my heart to Jesus."

Topaz choked on iced tea and wiped his eyes. "Come on, you crazy thing, let's pick up some Tums and hit the road."

Arden raised an eyebrow to signal Glenda and said in a stage whisper that resounded throughout the cafe, "My brother is ready for the check now."

Chapter 2
Physics

Bobbi June Kilgore stirred under the covers. In her left ear she felt intense heat, then her chest caught fire. Heat traveled from zone to zone throughout her body. Carefully, so as not to wake her husband, she slid a torrid foot over into the next zone, the zone of cool, then slipped a hand into air conditioned arctic. There.

Maybe, she thought, this was the law of thermal dynamics. That a part of a body slipped into a new zone gradually took on the temperature of whatever might be around it. Sometimes Bobbi June's mind just astonished her. Wasn't it Einstein that invented thermal dynamics and other secrets of the universe? Time and space and all that?

It had been a waste of time and money sending her brother Lamar to college when it was the girls in the family had all the brains. Bobbi June and Thelma Raye had to get by on just high school and a year of what was called business college but was really just secretarial school. They had both made something of themselves anyway—Thelma Raye in Amway and herself in real estate—and here she was now, just a little old girl from Waycross, Georgia practically inventing physics.

Here came another flash, like she was in the burning pit for sure. She almost flung off the covers but stopped herself just in time. Billy Wayne needed his beauty sleep. She eased herself out of bed.

Nobody could appreciate the life of a dean without being one. Honest to Jesus it seemed like life was a lot simpler when Billy Wayne was just a plain old mathematics professor instead of dean of academic affairs like he was now. But she couldn't complain about the money.

She silently opened the mirrored door of the closet, catching a glimpse of someone in pink baby dolls, her face crimson, her hair wild. She made her eyes go small and turned her attention instead to matters of fashion. She needed to look nice today. She had clients to see to. Important ones. VIP college folks. Bobbi June's mission in life was to match folks up with the right house. This required a lot of psychology, knowing people, how they thought and all. That and knowing houses. They were a lot alike, really, people and houses.

Take this house. The closets were too small. It would be lovely not to have to share this one with Billy Wayne, though truth to tell she had moved most of his clothes into the boys' closet when they went off to college.

She had raised her boys in this house.

Boys not like Lamar. Boys who called, remembered Mother's Day. Boys who had been raised right.

She held up her beige polyester skirt, studied it critically, remembered the broken zipper she had not mended, struggled to wedge it back into the depths.

Bobbi June was not ungrateful for what she had, even if she must now slide her clothes around in this dark, cramped closet when other faculty wives had walk-in closets and his-and-hers sinks in their bathrooms. This was not the fifties anymore but the seventies, and people wanted such things, regular people and not necessarily materialistic ones. After all, houses were what she was all about, professionally speaking.

She and Billy Wayne might ought to buy them one of those cute condos out at the golf course. In fact that could just be the ticket for the new English professor she was meeting this morning, though of course Bobbi June would have to meet her first to determine her needs. To make a good match and all.

Would her Big Bend Realty blazer go with this skirt? She fanned out her blue pleated skirt across her knee. Maybe not. Stick to what she knew for sure. Besides, mixing blues was risky. White was nice for summer and went with everything. Put it together with that new little shell she bought last week at Southern Inspirations. Gold was a neutral color.

She hung her clothes on the outside of the closet and went on into the bathroom, where—as she had known all along—she must see herself fully and without mercy, like she was a stranger to her own self. That plump body might be cherubic. Billy Wayne liked it well enough, but then Billy Wayne was a lot more interested in his newspaper and his riding mower.

An advantage maybe. She leaned in and examined her face. No eyebrows. She and Thelma Raye had plucked them all out years ago at their very first slumber party. The weight of her cheeks was slowly taking the rest of her face on down with it. Like the Titanic. This was definitely not the face of a realtor who with just one more sale would become a member of the Million Dollar Club.

Not yet, it wasn't.

This might take a little time, but Bobbi June Kilgore knew exactly what she was doing. She glanced over to the tile counter where her makeup was arranged in rows like the starting team for Florida State at kick-off. Then she glanced into the bedroom at Billy Wayne's digital clock that told the numbers in red, like time was an everlasting emergency. It said 9:14. Maybe she should give a quick call over to the Dixie Court Motel and tell Miss Benbow—Dr. Benbow, she corrected herself—that she was running a tad late.

Why ever Dr. Benbow was staying at that old run down Dixie Court Motel on the wrong side of Tallahassee, a place where half the affairs in three towns were carried on, or used to be anyway, was more than Bobbi June could say. The place looked now like something out of that Alfred Hitchcock movie, the one where after seeing it, everybody she knew was scared to death of their own showers.

She sat down on the toilet, musing, glad nobody had made a movie yet about *that*. What was the name of the motel now, that one in the movie? Shoot, she was losing her memory too.

"Bates Motel," she said, retrieving the detail. Those Crumb boys ought to sell that old Dixie Court to Hollywood, sure enough. Nobody in their right mind nowadays would stay there unless they were cheap or poor.

Or crazy, she added, folding the toilet paper into neat squares. Couldn't be the money, though. The college had agreed to pay Miss Benbow a generous salary, lord knows, because that's what minorities went for, Billy Wayne had said, when you could find you one at all. And the college had been under the gun on account of all that flap with the board. Or rather *one person* on the board. So they found them a nice Mexican lady with a PhD.

Bobbi June flushed and turned on the shower. Lord, it was a shame the way one or two people could ruin things for just everybody.

But the tepid water on her back, her shoulders, her breasts, flooded optimism back into her mind and spirit. Bobbi June, like her mama, was a born optimist. And now that she thought about it, she remembered a very nice Mexican man when she was a little girl in Waycross. A professional man too, a doctor. Everybody just loved him to death. Dr. Garcia, that was it. He kept his lawn nice and eventually married Ouida Wylie of Cairo. Two pretty girls, they had, with those nice olive complexions that she personally would kill for. Both girls had married well, to nice boys, boys who had made something of themselves.

And so maybe now everybody would like Miss Benbow too. *Dr.* Benbow, she corrected herself. For some reason it was important to academics that you doctor them. Well, shoot, they had worked hard for that degree. Billy Wayne sure had, and not just Billy Wayne, but she, Bobbi June, had worked hard for his degree too, being what her mama had always told her she should be, the woman behind the man.

It was nice that women were getting to be doctors now, too, themselves though, like this Dr. Benbow. Being a woman and a Mexican made her what Billy Wayne called a two-fer, meaning two for the price of one and so a bargain. They had been lucky to land her, competition being what it was today. Billy Wayne said money talked, but Bobbi June thought, shoot, why wouldn't she want to come to a town as nice as Midway? Folks were friendly here.

Bobbi June turned off the shower, stepped dripping onto the pink bath mat, then wrapped herself in a thick pink towel.

At her dressing table, applying the foundation, she could see as if in a magic mirror Midway rolling out the red carpet for the new poetry professor. Why in ten or twenty years, everybody in town would consider her practically one of them. Like Dr. Garcia in Waycross.

Dr. Benbow would be pretty. (Bobbi June penciled on her eyebrows.) If not pretty, then certainly stylish, coming from California and all. High cheekbones, like that Rita Moreno in the movies, or maybe it was Carmen Miranda she was thinking of. A woman you could admire. Foreign but in a good, maybe mysterious way. She might tilt her chin just so and look off into space like she could hear faraway music or a dog whistle.

Everybody was going to just love her to death.

An hour and twenty minutes later Bobbi June Kilgore wheeled her garnet and gold Lincoln Town Car into the parking lot of the Dixie Court Motel and cut the ignition. She felt strangely uncomfortable, as if someone were observing her from behind a curtain. Anthony Perkins, or worse yet, his mother.

She had driven all the way from her lovely home in Midway to this disreputable hotel in Tallahassee carrying in the locket of her mind a picture of Dr. Arden Benbow, but the woman she saw now under the beat-up aluminum umbrella did not match up. This woman had a large nose, straight, unstyled black hair and an unladylike laugh, none of which would mean very much at all—for Bobbi June was no stranger to disappointment—if Dr. Benbow had not been doing the laughing in the company of a tall, handsome Negro man wearing a pith helmet and very dark glasses, who hung on her every word like he could just eat her up.

Bobbi June was not naive. Bobbi June knew these people were together and in love and were husband and wife. She had seen such things before, of course, but not in a way that made her responsible and accountable for it. Bobbi June felt limb struck.

It was certainly heating up in the Town Car. A rivulet of sweat stole down her left temple and dropped like a tear onto the shoulder of her polyester blazer. Was another hot flash catching up to her? Emotional distress could bring one on, according to *Reader's Digest*. The article she had said instead of trying to talk your body out of it, to go right ahead with it instead. It said to pretend you were on a surfboard in Hawaii waiting to catch the wave. By trying hard and being creative instead of negative, you could ride the wave on in and wash ashore feeling calm, in control, fulfilled.

For a strange moment it seemed there might be something natural about all this—the hot flash, the man, the woman, the wave. Calm might be possible. But once this thought insinuated itself into her body, she knew it to be wrong, selfish. She had to get a grip on herself, think of the college and her Billy Wayne.

She took four deep breaths, mopped her brow with her hanky and watched the couple under the umbrella. It was a natural fact that Dr. Benbow could not exactly be white, since she was Mexican and all. But if she wasn't white, then what color was she, and who was it all right for her to be with in that kind of way? The way a man and woman naturally were.

Bobbi June couldn't get her hands on the surfboard of equilibrium, much less ride it safely up onto the beach of tranquility. Maybe she did need hormones, like her sister kept telling her. It was not fair that all this should fall to her, a woman with no college degree at all, only a Florida Realtor's license. Somehow she had become the first line of defense for the college. She who was not a dean and never would be.

But she could not stay inside this oven of a car, nor could she drive away and leave her Billy Wayne in danger. She was not stupid. She knew he had enemies, people just waiting for a chance to see him left grinning like a jackass eating briars. These chickens would come to roost. Being a dean was like that, he had told her often enough. No, Bobbi June Lumley Kilgore—like all the Lumley women before her—would stand by her man. Resolute, she swung wide the door of her Lincoln Town Car onto the bright scene and bid the strangers welcome.

Chapter 3

Grits

"You want some salt and pepper for that, Topaz honey? Ketchup?" Bobbi June leaned across the table at Mike's Cafe. The man had been staring down into his grits like they were a bucket of snakes. "Is it all right to call you by your first name, Mr. Wilson, honey?"

Too late she realized she had broken one of her mama's cardinal rules of etiquette and asked a question at the very moment Mr. Wilson had overcome, perhaps only temporarily, his dread of grits. His fork was better than halfway to his mouth.

But Dr. Benbow lightly took up for him the burden of conversation. Maybe she would work out after all. "Let's not stand on ceremony, Bobbi June," she told her. "And you can call me Arden. You're the first person ever to call me Dr. Benbow, and every time you do, I think for just a minute I might be wanted in surgery."

"Well, Arden honey," Bobbi June said, whipping her two eggs over light blithely into her grits, "what kind of a residence did y'all have in mind? And were you thinking of living in Tallahassee and commuting to Midway? I don't know but what you'd be better off right here in the capital city, where folks are a tad more liberal minded."

She glanced anxiously in Topaz's direction. It might just be the grits, but he looked to her like he was having a hard time swallowing. Bobbi June struggled to read him. The couple in the booth opposite seemed to be watching sideways the unfolding drama, though they were too polite and uptown to stare outright.

What did they see? She followed the line of their gaze to Dr. Benbow's left hand, gesturing with one of Mike's biscuits as she talked about her attraction to grass and leaves and such. "Whatever is green," Dr. Benbow was saying, and suddenly Bobbi June fixed her keen blue eyes on that ring finger, that carefully pared, colorless and totally naked ring finger.

They were not married, she realized with a jolt. Not married and not engaged to be. It probably was the farthest thing from their minds.

Bobbi June felt something like fear for them. She thought of the gazelles in last night's TV nature film just before the lion broke through the grass and chased them out into the open. She closed her eyes at the recollection, closed them down tight, but on the backs of her eyelids images of rent flesh and torn cartilage flashed their warnings anyway. When she opened her eyes back up, her two clients were staring at her with expressions of curiosity and maybe even concern.

She smiled back at them so they could enjoy their eggs and grits, but her own appetite just like the gazelle on TV was dead in its tracks. Her clients seemed almost simple, not exactly simple-minded, but simple. Like they did not understand all the ways folks could figure out to be spiteful as fire ants, if you riled them. Even the people at the college, educated as they were.

What could be done? Certainly these were the seventies and a live-and-let-live attitude seemed to be creeping its way toward them from both coasts, but it had not arrived yet in northwest Florida. The kind of change these folks needed could take decades. They did not know that, her clients. They seemed not to notice everybody was staring, that things were different here in the South.

Maybe they would set the date as soon as they realized people here did not do things like they do in California and maybe never would.

She buttered her biscuit, then set it down on her plate and absently poured cane syrup on it, stared at it as if it was a scatter pin at a flea market, then used it to shovel grits onto her fork.

Dr. Benbow was going on about nature and some friend of hers named Walt, who, like her, was crazy about grass and whatever else was green. She might be winding down now.

"So, Bobbi June, I might save us all some time by saying I really think the children would be better off living out in the country somewhere."

"Children?" Bobbi June gulped.

"Six of them," said Mr. Wilson, signaling the waitress for more coffee.

The grits seemed somehow to have got sucked up into Bobbi June's eustachian tube. It took her half a glass of water and several slaps on the back to settle down.

"Well that is a lovely family," she gasped at last. "Six. My, now. You don't see that much any more. Used to you did."

"And of course there's also Alice," said Arden.

"Alice is your girl," added Bobbi June, dabbing at her imperiled eyeliner with a paper napkin.

"Alice is an adult." Dr. Benbow set down the pepper and looked offended.

"I meant Alice is your maid, honey. That's what I meant. That's what we mean when we say 'your girl'. It's just our way of talking." She rescued her biscuit from the egg-drenched grits, her red lacquered nails looking strange even to her own eyes, curving as they did around dough and cane syrup and butter. Her stomach had not been ready for all this.

"Actually," said Mr. Wilson, "*I'm* the maid."

"Alice is my lover," said Dr. Benbow.

Bobbi June felt herself seize up like the stuffed deer over the door to the bathrooms. She couldn't chew or swallow. All she could do was hold onto her biscuit as if it was a tiny life preserver and look off at the traffic going by the window. She might be having a stroke. Her brain was idling rough as that old riding mower of Billy Wayne's before she let him trade it in on the Snapper.

Meanwhile Dr. Benbow stared at her, not eating. Finally she looked Bobbi June straight in the eye and explained in her patient teacher voice, "Alice and I are married and have six children."

At least Bobbi June thought that was what the woman said. But it seemed like she was talking some kind of foreign language, one Bobbi June studied a long time ago and could only order simple meals in. "Married? To each other? Two women? Together? Why I didn't think that was possible."

"Well it isn't legal," said Mr. Wilson, slicing into his thick Bradley's country sausage, "and yet it certainly is possible."

"But the children. I don't see how—"

"Of course they must at one time have had a biological father, but sad to say that was not Topaz. Probably they continue to have a father."

"Lord have mercy," said Bobbi June, turning to Topaz Wilson. "Then who are you?"

"Topaz is my dearest friend," said Arden, buttering the last biscuit. "He kindly agreed to come along to keep me company and to help me house hunt. Then Alice and the children will join us."

"Join *you*," corrected Mr. Wilson. "I'm heading back to civilization after we find the dream house."

"Well my stars," said Bobbi June at last. "We simply had no idea. No idea at all. None of us."

"*We?*" said Arden.

"Well I say *we*, but I mean the college when I say that. My Billy Wayne being in a position of responsibility as dean of academic affairs and all."

"I can tell, Bobbi June, honey," said Arden, laying down her knife, "that our concept of family is exactly the same, yours and mine."

Bobbi June waited for a minute, as if Arden Benbow might be about to say more, explain just what she meant. But instead her new client ate with complete attention and satisfaction the rest of her biscuit, while Bobbi June had to pretend the flames that started in her chest were not rising up her neck and into her face, threatening what was left of her foundation.

Chapter 4
Crossroads

Six hours later Topaz Wilson lounged on the broken front steps of a broken-down plantation half a mile outside Midway, Florida, at the exact point where Lower Bridge Road crossed the Old Aaron Highway. Bobbi June had said this was where the two-rut road met the hard road, one leading off to an old shade tobacco farm and a dead town, the other to a viable mushroom farm and eventually, thought Topaz, if you played your cards just right, to California. He and Arden had got here on I-10. They could just as easily go back. Roads ran both ways, his old auntie used to say.

Topaz fanned himself with his limp tie. Why had he worn this? Somehow buying a house had seemed such a solemn occasion that he had dressed without realizing it as if for a funeral. His tie felt like a noose. Why would anybody want to own a house? He was a renter at heart and by birth. Anything went wrong, call the landlady on your way out the front door. Landladies, to him, were minor gods, except if they didn't make things right you could always move.

And this climate. Humans could not have been intended to live here. The June sun drilled through branches of ancient live oak draped in sheets of Spanish moss. He felt as if someone's large and ancient foot were resting directly on his chest. Tradition, he wondered? This had been a plantation, after all. A real one.

"Is this what's known as humidity?" he asked Bobbi June, testing his ability to speak at all in this strange new atmosphere. Their realtor sat collapsed on the porch swing next to Arden. Together the three of them had looked at thirteen houses since breakfast. The older woman's sprayed hair was stoved in a little on the left side of her head, and her eyes had long since lost their focus, not to mention their luster. Behind her, the Town Car rested like an exhausted horse, though the spirited motto on its heaving side boasted in jaunty gold letters—BIG BEND REALTY: WE SELL FLORIDA.

Earlier Topaz had noticed a bumper sticker on the back bumper that said "Seminole Fever" as if warning against some kind of communicable disease. "Football," Bobbi June had explained, "you know, at the state university. I'm talking about Florida State, honey. Football is the local religion in these parts."

Text seemed to adhere to Bobbi June, or perhaps to the whole South. Bumper stickers, placards, billboards, illuminated signs with crucial letters missing—all of them giving advice on how to live right. He and Arden had better learn to read this new language, something told him, or they would not survive. The thought was exhausting.

"We call it *hu-ma-ditty*," Bobbi June called back in a last ditch effort at playfulness. "You'll get used to it quick enough, sugar pie."

"Not if I can help it," said Topaz, mopping his brow with the end of his tie.

"I like it," said Arden. "I really do. The air here has substance, heft, a corporeal presence. There's grace in that. Solid air. Just imagine it's enfolding you in its arms."

"What's enfolding you, Arden honey?"

"The moist body of Florida herself."

Bobbi June snorted. "That's a good one."

Topaz struggled to rise, gave up and said, "So Arden, what's it going to be? Bobbi June here has got to get on home to Bobby Wayne. She's tired and so am I."

"It's *Billy* Wayne. I like to say, I'm Bobbi, he's Billy, but we're both Kilgores. Well, actually I'm a Lumley, but I'm a Kilgore too now, I guess."

"I've always found questions of identity a little exhausting," Arden said, fanning herself with a Big Bend Realty brochure.

"Not in my experience," said Topaz. "You *like* questions of identity or you wouldn't be here at all."

"And that's just where a good house can come in at," said Bobbi June as if intercepting a forward pass. "Nothing like a nice residence to hold you in and let you know who you are. Lets the world know it too. I can't think what I would have done without my nice brick house Billy Wayne built for me. I raised my two boys in that house."

She glanced over at Topaz, then back at Arden. "Just listen at me, will you? I've been going on and on. But part of me the whole time has been thinking about y'all and your special needs. I call it my *bidness* mind, the part that ticks on like a steel clock while my other mind keeps up with conversation. Looks to me like y'all'd be much happier in Tallahassee than you ever could be way out here. Perfect strangers all alone in a little biddy town with—"

"Little biddy minds," finished Topaz. "Listen to the woman, Arden. She knows what she's talking about."

"But I don't want to live in Tallahassee. I want to live here."

"*Right* here?" gasped Topaz. "You mean in this very house, the one with no roof and not much floor? You mean this house which was raised up by black slaves and possibly Indians as well, to whom—who knows? You might even have been related. You mean you want to live with your innocent babes and your devoted spouse in this dilapidated monument to the most vicious impulses of European patriarchy?"

"And what better place!" declared Arden, as if Topaz has proved her very point. "We'll take back this monument and claim it in the name of La Malinche."

"Who's Malinchey?" asked Bobbi June. "Is she from around here? Who are her people?"

Topaz knew in his bones Arden was going to answer this question, that for her no question was negligible. "Malinche is dead," he offered, hoping to put an end to it but not expecting to.

"Dead?" said Bobbi June. "Oh I am so sorry for your loss."

"History is not dead," said Arden, a little circle of pink appearing in each of her brown cheeks. "Malinche was the Aztec princess who interpreted for Cortés. She's the goddess of language and patron saint to all women poets, the first activist, sometimes called La Chingada, which in English translates as—"

"Malinche'd want screens on her damn windows and Alice will too," Topaz interrupted. "Trust me."

"Use your imagination, Topaz. See a new roof on it, tin possibly, the floors repaired and refinished, the porch spruced up, windows fixed, a little paint. Okay, a *lot* of paint. But we need eight bedrooms. Where else is this family going to find eight bedrooms?"

"Alice wants eight bathrooms too. Don't forget that. This house has got one big strange one. An afterthought in plumbing."

"We'll add a couple. How hard could it be? And we could raise all our own food right here, be self-sustaining. They did it once. This was a working plantation. We can all learn to garden. The kids will love it."

"Aside from an occasional air fern I can't say I've ever seen you grow anything of consequence. Not the way you mean. You're a poet. You sow language. You reap images."

"Exactly. Metaphors acknowledge real similarities between two things, connections that may seem bizarre but really aren't. Like maybe all poets are gardeners."

"You killed the ficus."

"I did not *kill* the ficus. I witnessed its death. Something else poets have in common with gardeners. We both chronicle death. Now let's go see the yard. It can't hurt to look."

"I'll wait right here. Moving around takes more air."

"I'll go with you, Arden honey," said Bobbi, struggling to her feet.

"This is a real nice piece of land for the right person. It might not have much curb appeal, but anybody with one eye and half sense could see this place has got real hidden potential. I know Malinchey would of liked it—if she had lived to see it—and Alice will too."

Arden studied admiringly the three live oaks and stand of pines running along the western property line. A hawk high up in the blank afternoon sky lazily caught updrafts. Arden had found, just this side of that first oak tree, a perfect spot for her windmill. In her poet's mind the blades already revolved slowly, pumping fresh spring water toward the tender plants of her garden. Children, her own and dozens she had yet to meet, bent to the joyous labor, the sound of their garden tools working through the earth symphonic, their voices bright with expectation.

"How much land did you say, Bobbi June?" she asked, turning suddenly toward her realtor.

"Well, used to, it was eighteen hundred acres. I'm just trying to think what it's down to now. I believe it's about eight acres, give or take. It says just exactly in my book back there in the car. We'll check it out. Got us a good survey done when the property first went on the market back in . . ." She trailed off, but Arden did not notice.

Arden *had* noticed something else, though. An outbuilding connected to the house by a covered walkway, an umbilicus. "I don't remember seeing that added-on part, Bobbi June."

"Lord, that's not another thing in this world but one of those big old-fashioned kitchens, honey, hooked onto the big house by a dogtrot. We didn't bother going in there because of it needing so much work and Mr. Topaz being so tired and out of sorts. Probably it was a storehouse last anybody used it. A little elbow grease and you could probably fix you up a nice little playhouse for those girls of yours. Folks built them off by themselves so as not to catch the house on fire, if there was a blaze. Cooler too in the summer."

Arden paused, contemplating the old kitchen as a possible studio, a place to write without catching the house on fire. Then she turned and noticed off across the overgrown garden plot another house, one that looked like her kitchen but larger, with a porch across the whole front. "And who lives over there?"

"That's part of the less I was talking about, Arden honey. That old cabin on its little bit of land sticks right on into yours, kind of like a little island, you might say."

"A peninsula," corrected Arden, gazing at the nest-like porch, vacant now.

"That's Miss Hattie's place. She lives there and has for as long as anybody can remember. Hattie White. Children are all grown and scattered to the winds. Got their college, then nothing could hold them back. Nobody much coming by to look in on her, far as I know, except somebody from her little church every now and again to carry her to the IGA and such. 'Course mostly she eats straight from that garden of hers. That's it right next to the house there." Bobbi June pointed. "Just look at those Floradel tomatoes! Folks could take a lesson. Say, she might could give you some advice, get you started, like.

"That little house of hers was part of the original plantation, Daddy says, slave cabin most likely. But after the war Mrs. Faircloth, she up and give Miss Hattie's mama that house free and clear, to stay in her family right along. Now it belongs to Miss Hattie. She's got an easement across your land so she can have lawful access by that little footpath there and a little bit of swampy land behind that doesn't amount to much. Miss Hattie's a nice old lady, don't bother nobody. Just sits on that porch of hers rocking and watching the world go right on by."

Arden shaded her eyes. As she stood contemplating, an old black woman in a print housedress came out on the porch carrying a green bowl, leaning on a walking stick. She returned their gaze for a moment, then settled herself on into her rocker.

"Shelling her up a mess of butter beans," said Bobbi June, then gave herself a little shake back to the business at hand. "Look, Arden honey, I'm not going to beat all about the bush with you, 'cause I like you. Plenty of folks wouldn't want this old place just because of the neighborhood, so to speak. You know what I'm saying? But shoot, I say that's what makes it so affordable, that and being a fixer-upper of course."

Then the two women heard someone calling from behind and turned to see Topaz picking his way across the field toward them, tie pressed to his brow. "Consider, Arden! Think twice, I'm telling you. Owning anything is tricky business. Ask Malinche. Ask Alice."

Arden turned to look deep into her realtor's flushed and earnest face. "So tell me, Bobbi June, just exactly how much is it?"

Chapter 5
Simultaneity

"Say what you will, Alice," said Chowder, ratcheting in the sheet line and coming about neatly, "Arden's just not a good fit."

"You've always said so," remarked Alice, staring off toward Catalina Island and looping her hair neatly behind her ears. "But then ex-husbands are likely to be hard on their successors."

"Hold the tiller, will you dear, while I get us a beer?" He disappeared down the hatch, then popped up again holding a bottle of beer in one hand and a bottle of champagne in the other, smiling in that way that always reminded Alice of some Kennedy or other. She nodded toward the champagne, and he took her meaning quickly as spouses will or even, as in this case, former spouses. When he returned on deck, he balanced the bottle of champagne and two plastic tulip glasses. A corkscrew peeped out of his breast pocket.

"Besides," said Alice, taking the extended glasses in one hand, "what do you mean by fit? If you mean as an academic, then I might agree with you. But if you mean as a mate, my mate, then you'd better look around for another topic of conversation." She eased out the sheet line, and the boat leapt ahead.

Chowder steadied himself and took his place in the cockpit. "My dear Alice," he said, twisting in the corkscrew, "I mean far, far more than I can explain in the hour we've got left today, nor is Miss Benbow, or should I say *Dr.* Benbow, my favorite topic of conversation. But let's just say I have difficulty imagining her at an institution of higher learning, teaching poetics to tomorrow's citizens and artisans. Teaching requires nurturing, if I'm not mistaken." He extracted the cork, leaned close to Alice and carefully filled one of the glasses. "Now it's true, apparently, that she's the mother of six children. Malthus says so, and he should know."

"I don't lose sight of the fact that you're Malthus's friend. You see things from his perspective."

"Well, yes, and you see things from hers. The man's about to lose his children."

"The man has access to the same telephones, planes and trains that you do. His rights are protected by decree and by Arden's commitment to their well-being and mine too, as you certainly know." She gazed to windward.

"I'm already persuaded that you have a very refined sense of responsibility." She returned his gaze. He looked away and began pouring champagne carefully into his own glass. "It's hers I'm worried about. Without you, she couldn't keep a houseplant alive, let alone the six kids. I mean where is she now, right this minute? Two time zones away, that's where."

"She's house-hunting," corrected Alice, sipping her wine and ignoring Chowder's invitation to a toast. "She's trying to find a house for us with enough bedrooms, doors and bathrooms. Surely that's a nurturing act. Now prepare to come about."

Chowder protected his glass and ducked his head to avoid the swinging boom. "And who, pray, is with her children right now?" He settled himself again next to Alice and drained his glass.

Alice consulted her watch. "If you mean *our* children, Kip's at cornet lessons, Hillary's selling Girl Scout cookies, Jamie's—"

"Spare me," he interrupted, laughing. "But who's in *charge*?"

"Well, Tom, more or less. He's spelling me this afternoon."

"Exactly, my dear. Somehow she's assembled an entire crew of child-care workers, among which she does not herself number. No, she doesn't fit as a mother, and I'm damned if I can visualize her as a faculty member of a college. She's not house-hunting either, my dear. Odds are she's getting herself tattooed this very minute. Here, hold them steady."

"Doubt it," said Alice, propping the tiller against her knee and holding the glasses for refilling.

"And now," he said, pouring carefully, "she's traipsed halfway across the country, no, *all* the way across the country. Florida, my God! It's a cultural abyss."

"I've never been there," said Alice brightly. "Have you?" She fixed him with her keen brown eyes and handed him his glass.

"Besides, there's your job to consider. You know very well a lot of hard work went into that vice presidency they've offered you."

Alice lifted her glass in acknowledgment of the compliment; his plastic glass met hers.

"Umm. This is really very good," he said, settling back against the cushion. "It's that Mumm's you like so much."

She nodded, checked the compass.

He frowned.

She lifted her eyebrows.

"I was just thinking, dear, you've got to remember that you're not getting any younger. Arden, on the other hand, is."

"You're very negative today, with this silly disquisition on Arden as misfit. You're just cranky because I'll be going away where we won't be able to go sailing occasionally or lunch at Farmer's Market now and then. Now don't go looking like that. There are, after all, the afore-mentioned telephones, telegrams, trains, mail and, yes, even airplanes. Florida is not the end of the world. Probably."

"Alice, you're forty-eight."

"Seven," Alice corrected gently. She tipped back her head and emptied the glass.

Chapter 6
Survey

Arden stood alone on the front steps of the house of her dreams while Topaz slept in at the Dixie Court Motel, exhausted by yesterday's quest for the home place. Dark clouds rolled across the summer sky from last night's storm, and a mist emanated from the woods as from the collective breath of awakening trees. Birds whose songs she did not yet know called and swooped and invited.

This morning she had managed to talk Bobbi June into relinquishing the key and granting her privacy. She needed to see the place alone, when everything was quiet. So she could calculate space. And need and desire. After all, she must choose for Alice and the children, not just for herself. She was aware she tended to get carried away and that this transport had a kinship to wonder, and so she must somehow quell wonder, at least temporarily. Instead she felt around inside her brain to see if she had a counterpart to Bobbi June's "bidness mind." It must be in there somewhere, she thought, fitting the key into the lock and swinging open the front door.

It was hard to believe a house this size could cost so little, she thought, walking into the foyer. Alice had hardly believed it herself, when they talked last night on the phone. Eight bedrooms, a music room, a sun-room, a sewing room, a parlor, a living room. Different rooms for dif-ferent needs, a house shaped by a family's requirements rather than an architect's aesthetics. But what need did a parlor satisfy? California had never seemed to have parlors except now and then in movies.

As she stood musing, excitement manifested itself in the illusion of movement on her ankles and calves. A quick glance down puzzled her. She did not recall having put on black knee-high socks this morning, in this blistering heat. And as she looked she realized the socks were com-posed of a million moving dots, living creatures with obscure motives all their own.

She ran through the house in search of water, some autonomic sys-tem in her brain telling her that water might stop the swarming fleas from driving her mad. No water at the kitchen sink. She turned and bounded up the stairs searching for the strange-looking bathroom, not sure which door led where, the house suddenly a labyrinth, un-til yes, there it was, just as she had remembered, four inches of rusty water standing in the giant, claw-footed bathtub, courtesy of deus ex machina.

Ah, tepid water lapped her ankles while thousands of fleas released their hold. She eased off her soggy Keds and tossed them overboard onto the buckled linoleum, stood, contemplating her fate. At thirty-eight, she could observe with some equanimity that there had always been vermin in paradise. Nothing came unalloyed. All energy emanated from the spark struck by the sudden abrasion of the actual against the ideal.

Outside the window a pine gently fingered the side of the house. She took in a deep breath. And then let it out. She was home. Home in the profoundest sense. Morning light elbowed aside clouds, illuminating her face and one arm.

She dreamed of Aztlán, the mythic lost land of the Aztecs, her people, their dear homeland that might be in New Mexico, Arizona, Utah or . . . or some people—respectable scholars, as she recalled—had even placed it somewhere in Florida. Had they not? Yes, she was almost positive, quite positive, they had. One crack-brained theory put it in Wisconsin. Clearly, that was absurd. But Florida. Now that was really quite plausible. Likely, even. Aztlán. And she, Arden Benbow, had returned to claim on behalf of all the earth's dispossessed the archetypal homeland for her people and to do so in the name of Malinche, first mother of language and confused identity.

She stepped lightly out of the tub, picked up her shoes, smacked them together smartly, ready to continue her survey. Glancing left, she designated the large bedroom at the front with the cross ventilation as the mistress suite, and on the same floor—she continued down the hall—this small, airy room across the hall could be for Ellen, nearly five now, the next for Max, just turned seven. Maybe put Hillary in this room with the window seat, for recently adolescence had inclined her to a *Wuthering Heights* view of life.

On the other hand, they would need another live-in helper, if Topaz planned truly to leave. But how could he abandon them? How could he go? Four years ago he had answered her ad for a live-in mother's helper. He had organized their family life and in exchange they had welcomed him as a member. But now, he had received his MFA in dance, and she had received her PhD in poetry.

Unwittingly they had graduated, thereby creating the expectation in others that they had all along been preparing themselves for important work. And here she was this morning in this strange Florida, the one the local radio announcer called "the land of muckworms." What were muckworms anyway, and how could Topaz consider leaving her in such a place?

She stopped herself in this way of thinking, sinking down onto the window seat. Her love for him wanted whatever he believed best. The problem with motherhood was that it inclined you to think that you alone could keep the whole pack running in the right direction by virtue of your experienced nipping and yipping at their flying heels. Survival lent an imperative to this motherly frenzy. Years of living with the specter of Malthus and the possibility of losing custody of her children to him had led to crisis thinking.

But now, she thought, resting her hand in the plank of sunlight on the bench beside her, she had a job and a three-thousand-mile buffer zone between her and Malthus. She must learn to accept the blessing of safety. Here in this house at the crossroads, they might all be free. And she would learn to step back now, allowing each of them to stretch in the Florida sun and strike out in whatever direction beckoned.

Still, her business mind observed, bringing her back to the present moment, the fact of this wonderful room with the window seat might lead Topaz to reconsider. Definitely she would save it for him on the off chance. And it was so perfectly located near the strange bathroom, too, though she knew in his fastidiousness he would want his own, his very own.

They all would. Strange humankind with their insistence on bathrooms! And for a moment she felt she might not be able to satisfy all their curious and often inexplicable needs. Forthwith she resigned as mother of the world. At least, the American world, for saner countries did not worship plumbing. Yes, she would resign the great mother position to become instead steward of the land, trustee of the philosophy that a little deep hoeing and judicious fertilizing would produce, in this life, plenty for everybody.

She climbed the stairs to the third floor. The ceiling plunged low at the edges for she must be in the attic, but there were generous windows at either end, and yes, here it was—the world's smallest bathroom! You could sit on the toilet and wash your hands at the same time. A tiny metal shower with a rusty floor and one handle missing. No, here it was, stuck in the drain. Put the elder kids up here: Arthur, Kip, Hillary and Jamie. None of them threatened to be very tall anyway.

And that did it. She counted back on her hands. Yes, all six had her or his own room. Two bathrooms, one large, one small. Put another in on the first floor, and all their needs would be met perfectly.

Speaking of which, now would be the ideal time to check out her writing room, the little birth pod clinging to the back of the house. She thundered down the two flights of stairs, crossed the hall, and found the dogtrot through a narrow door in the kitchen. She would hang her Thinking Hammock right here at the entrance to her writing room. She liked the uneven feel of these old boards beneath her feet, though some of them needed replacing.

The door to the pod resisted, then gave way. Morning sun flooded through the east window. Smaller windows on the north and south let in oblique light, and there might be a window on the other side, concealed under that mismatched bead board. If not, she could always add one. An electrical outlet snaked halfway up the wall. Mentally she placed her desk before the big window on the east wall. Outside, a spray of flaming blossoms pressed against the window as if seeking entry, then cascaded down onto the wild and knotty grass below.

From this room great poems would blossom, springing forth from the roots she would soon set down into this fecund Florida soil. For a moment she rested a finger lovingly on the blistered white paint of the window ledge, as on the pulse of a dear one, then crossed the room and languidly descended the two short steps from the dogtrot into the side yard. She gazed up into an old live oak draped in Spanish moss, through which morning sun streamed, steamed and shimmered.

How could she possibly resist stretching high into blue Florida sky to pull down a strand of the moss and wind it into her long California hair?

Chapter 7
Square Root

Arden sat uneasily in the back of Dean Billy Wayne Kilgore's black Mercedes doing breathing exercises to control the furious itching in her scalp. Her first lesson on the local flora and fauna had revealed somewhat dramatically the symbiotic relationship between Spanish moss and chiggers. The night clerk at the Dixie Court Motel had expertly diagnosed both the problem and the treatment. Alas, the Chigger Rid offered temporary relief but only time could cure. With a pair of blunt nose Raggedy Ann scissors extracted from the hearse's glove compartment at two that morning, Topaz had, with some art, trimmed her long dark mane down to a startled looking patch more easily penetrated by the Chigger Rid.

What was hair, after all, but an accretion of dead cells to be sloughed off one way or another? Transformation was but another word for life. She was growing new hair now, while Dean Billy Wayne drove them on this tour of the campus and Topaz, bless him, made polite conversation in the front seat. She scratched one of her welts and resolved to do her part to sustain conversation.

"It's good we're taking your car, Billy Wayne," said Topaz. "Ours is starting to mildew. We left our windows down yesterday when we went for lunch."

"A real gully washer, eh?" laughed Billy Wayne.

"The floor mats were floating," added Arden.

"Well, you'll learn quick enough what you can and can't do around here."

Had he intended something? Was his apparently chance remark a coded warning? Was she being paranoid? In the presence of authority figures she had always tended to gnash her teeth. But this was a new chapter altogether, she reminded herself, and she, a new person. She would leave off old ways, accepting both chiggers in paradise and yes, even deans in academe.

This one had been talking incessantly, though in a tone light enough for anybody. "Bobbi June tells me you're considering purchasing the old Faircloth Plantation. Not a bad idea. I guess if you told anybody in California they could buy an eight bedroom, thirty-five hundred-odd square foot house on seven and a half rolling acres for seventy-nine thousand they'd think you were teasing. 'Course it's going to need a little of what my B. J. calls TLC. She means tender loving care. I say it means tender like crazy. You know, legal tender? But I guess if you're careful you'll make it."

Arden studied herself in the dean's rearview mirror. Was that her? *She*, rather? Her head, a stubbly field? Was he waiting for her to speak, to comment on the wisdom of such a philosophy? The philosophy of caution. If I'm careful I'll make it. She ground her teeth and said in a controlled tone, "I'm pretty handy, actually."

The dean seemed not to have heard. His eyes swung over to Topaz. "The missus says you're moving on. That right Topaz, if I may call you that?"

"You may and I am. Soon as we close on the house and get that U-Haul unloaded. I'm starting to feel like it's grafted onto my body. I walk with a lurch now. I might say a *hitch*. See there, I've succumbed to trailer park humor."

"Well, Arden, if you do decide on the Faircloth place, you might ought to hire you some locals to do the work. Come September, you're going to be one busy lady. 'Course, starting a new job is always demanding, but Midway College has plans for you that you may not be aware of."

He stopped at a red light, and heavy drops began to pelt the windshield. Soon the whole car was encased in sheets of rain. The sound of the engine was lost in the roar of water on the roof. The dean must have been blinded by the downpour, yet his car rolled on resolutely toward the Administration Building.

"You see, Arden—and Topaz, you can listen too—Midway College has a mission." He raised his voice uncomfortably, almost shouting at the blank windshield. "Now as you know, we've got a pretty fair endowment for an institution our size. You've benefited from that already. 'Course you haven't started actually drawing your paycheck yet, but you know what I'm talking about."

He turned around in his seat and sought out her eyes while the car moved forward, unguided. She felt a panicked impulse to fling herself over the front seat and grab the wheel out of his hands. But in another moment he turned his eyes back to the wash of the windshield and picked up the thread of his narration, his language a strange mixture of academic and Southern idiosyncrasies. The man, she reminded herself, did live after all with Bobbi June.

"What I'm talking about is putting Midway College into the top ten small liberal arts colleges within the next decade." He pulled up in front of the Administration Building—not incidentally the largest edifice on campus—running the engine, the air conditioning, his monologue. The car throbbed. "That's what President Cager calls for. And we can do it too. But we know we can't do it without the help of our distinguished faculty. No, we aren't anything at all without our faculty."

Arden was beginning to wonder—somewhat ungrammatically and not for the first time—just exactly who "we" was and whether the students figured into this little equation at all. Behind a curtain of rain, the concrete and windowless Administration Building hunched gloomily, perhaps hungrily.

"That's why we want to make you happy. Pay you a generous wage, benefits. And you're worth it. We know that. You're exceptional people, every last one of you. We appreciate you. I mean that sincerely. Now, you may be wondering just what we expect in return."

Arden had not given it a thought.

"What you can give in return is your undivided loyalty to Midway College and an unparalleled publication record."

"Publication?" said Arden, snapping to attention. "From what Professor St. John said at my MLA interview last December, I thought—"

"Oh, well yes, that's St. John's artistic view, and far be it from me to try to argue him out of it."

It was clear he had at least considered the possibility.

"St. John *is* the head of your program, and as such, obviously you owe him your allegiance, but the man does not believe poets should be required to publish. Gets in the way of art or some such. The man does not even believe writing can be taught, if I understand him correctly, but I notice he cashes his paychecks regularly enough.

"No," Dean Billy Wayne continued, a jet of cold air from the dash vent dislodging the strand of his hair delegated to the protection of his bald spot, "I would say St. John is just not a team player and so, from your point of view, not the man to emulate."

Arden had not meant to emulate any men at all.

"This is what you want to go for in managing your career: publish, publish, publish. I'd be remiss if I didn't tell you this. Then when you come up for tenure there won't be any question. Not that everyone is cut out for this kind of life. Academe has become competitive, like any business, but that's what keeps us on our toes. Survival, you might say, of the fittest. To the victor go the spoils and all like that."

The itching in her scalp had intensified. The dean's warning had suddenly driven blood to her head and thus fueled the flames. She felt married to Malthus again, for Malthus and the dean had in common the clear, familiar voice of assurance and authority, the voice of the eternally self-assured. Of he who knows and has the word, the mandate. An inherited, unthinking language of privilege. She had intended to divorce this voice, and in fact to divorce the whole culture that spawned it, but instead here she was now in the back seat of its Mercedes-Benz.

This man did not live by her newly articulated philosophy of plenty for everybody. In his philosophy there seemed only enough to fight over. Yet she would somehow have to live in the presence of his belief system, while clutching to her breast her own magnificent gods, her sacred trinity: Tonantzín, the divine mother; Coatlicue, goddess of transformation; and La Malinche, she of divided loyalties and ambiguous alliances.

Chapter 8
The Fourth Thing

"Now eat your toast, Billy Wayne, honey. You got to keep up your strength."

Billy Wayne was not hungry. Ever since Tuesday when Bobbi June had told him about the peculiarities of the new hire he had felt off his feed, as if creatures of some size were moving around in his stomach. And yesterday taught him she had not exaggerated. In fact things were worse even than she had said. After spending a couple of hours in the company of Dr. Benbow and her . . . her . . .

Words, like his stomach, keep failing him. His eye fell on the triangles of toast Bobbi June had arranged attractively on the Corelware, but they looked to him like four little white flags of surrender. He should be in charge here somehow. Take a position. A stand. But truth to tell, all he seemed able to do was sit here in his breakfast nook wearing his striped pajamas while his wife got ready for work.

Oh, in his mind he had got himself into his lightweight beige suit from Burdines and white, short sleeve shirt fresh from the laundry, lined up his pens in his breast pocket, picked up the telephone receiver behind him on the wall and calmly dialed a few numbers while he drank his coffee. Had called up Hazard, the chair of English, then the provost, even the president himself. But here the fantasy failed him. He didn't know how to even say what the problem was let alone suggest solutions.

Teaching mathematics had been different from this dean business, and there were days he wished he hadn't made the changeover, though he and Bobbi June never would have been able to afford the two boys in college at once—even with her working—if it hadn't been for this opportunity that had opened before him like a sudden break in traffic.

Startling him, Bobbi June bent down to kiss him goodbye. In his mind she had already left. He liked the way she smelled, all perfume and little purple soaps. For a minute she held him tight, like she might be going far away for a very long time, and then next thing he knew she was putting on her Big Bend Realty blazer and reminding him of the president's ball tonight. The door closed behind her and pretty soon he heard the engine start and the car whine backward down the drive and into the world. Billy Wayne took up his paper napkin and absently wiped the lipstick off his cheek.

Who would have dreamed she could sell anything? And yet here she was now, about to become a member of the Million Dollar Club and all because of this Faircloth Plantation deal edging her into the next higher circle of success. Nobody ever thought she'd pull it off, a sale like that. Now she was happy as a meadowlark, with no idea in the world that the same thing making her so goddamned happy was making him miserable as a pig at hog-killing time.

Women, he thought, you gotta love 'em. But you had to be eternally vigilant that the fragile craft of your shared domestic life was not headed for the rapids. That was the man's tough job.

Unbidden, the image of Arden Benbow rose before his eyes. Her hair whacked off in some kind of California fashion statement, standing up all over her head. She looked just like a possum caught in the beam of a flashlight. What was womanhood coming to anyhow?

It was true Bobbi June had become a career woman, but that was *it* for her. She would always be his own B. J., keeping a nice home for him and the boys to come back to. Up early and late, being cheerful, supporting him in his career just like it was her own. One flesh, the preacher had said, and amen to that.

He lifted his coffee cup and sipped, as if offering a toast to the preacher and to the perfect system that has made such comforts possible and available to him.

Cold. He swallowed the acrid liquid, got up, and dashed the contents of his cup into the sink. Plenty more where that came from. A little scorched maybe because of the lateness of the hour, but he was not particular. From the carafe he poured himself a new, hot cup, stirred in Cremora, which lumped on the oily surface. Three quick stirs and it sank out of sight, turning everything the right color. Now for two, may as well make it three teaspoons of sugar. Bobbi June wanted him to use that new stuff, Equal, but he told her like everything else with that name it was going to let you down in the end.

Maybe he had gone too far saying that. She had got all quiet on him. He could almost see her face. Startled, like. Then ready to go on to the next thing. A real trooper.

Being a mathematician did not mean that he was insensitive to women and their ways. Their feelings. Feelings that appeared unaccountably, suddenly, popping up everywhere like mushrooms in a pasture after a rainstorm. He glanced out the kitchen window at his grass. Checking it. Come Saturday he'd have to mow again. He could already envision himself moving in easy figure eights around his house, toward the woods, then back, alone and peaceful inside the steady sound of his new Snapper 3000.

He sat back down at the breakfast table and sighed. He'd have to stay focused on the problem at hand, do some real problem-solving here. If he sat around on his ass much longer this story of Benbow would break on its own. Matter of fact, he only had until the president's party tonight when Benbow's entrance would certainly tell the whole story quick enough. Then the provost would want to know why in hell he was the last to know, why he was *always* the last to know, the thing he hated most in this world.

So zero hour had arrived for Billy Wayne, and he would have to use some good hard logic, approach this like it was a problem in mathematics. A body could rely on mathematics. Or history even, his minor in college. Civil War. Because history was important here too. What his professor at Duke used to call "the vital context."

Well, the vital context was that Strickland, chairman of the board, had convinced them all they needed a minority hire, preferably a woman, that way killing two birds with one stone. So far so good. Strickland may have been right—better to act on this thing themselves before they started getting phone calls from parents in Des Moines. Might even have run into a legal problem on down the line, Strickland, who was a circuit court judge, had darkly hinted. Better to clean their own house than to let in a bunch of yahoos to do it for them later.

And that was when Booth Hazard had said the English department could use her on board because they only had two women and one was going on sabbatical and how would that look, just one woman and that one woman Bertha Michaels.

At the time it had seemed like the smart thing to do, and even lucky. Jane Oliver, just before she left on sabbatical, had reminded them that Mexican-American included Native American and so Benbow was by definition both. Or all three really, if you threw in there that she was a woman.

But here was the fourth thing and that was where all the trouble began. She was a l—a l—a l—He could not bring himself to say the word, not even inside his own mind where nobody was listening. How in the world was he going to call up anybody, sit there and babble at them like a complete fool? And who would he call anyway? And what were they going to do about it? What was *anybody* going to do about it?

They couldn't fire her for being a lesbian. *There, he had said it.* How would that look to the profession? His cross-town colleagues at Florida State, already sneering over Midway's flexible admission policies and generous salaries, would be quick to gossip about any new transgression against academic standards or liberal politics. Oh, they'd love to start rumors picturing Midway as the joke of the century. And just when

Midway had a good crack at getting into the private top ten, the way the president wanted. The way they *all* wanted. Then *this* had to happen.

No, they couldn't fire her. But they couldn't keep her either. Unless she could be persuaded to be discreet. Here he thought of Bertha Michaels fleetingly, then lost his train of thought because he liked Bertha, respected her. Arden Benbow, he could see, was another bird altogether. Moving into this quiet, conservative community and establishing high visibility—as she was about to do—right here at the Midway Crossroads, for all to see.

And his own wife had sold her the house. He could hardly believe it. The community was going to be up in arms, faculty up in arms, the board up in arms, parents up in arms. And most likely the parents would be *his* responsibility, the provost neatly sidestepping the whole thing so that the dirty work would fall to him. Again.

He guessed it was too much to hope for, that she'd just flat out decide this was not for her, that like St. John she would think competition might corrupt her poetry or some such. Just up and quit. Like that. Gone and out of their lives forever.

He had laid it on a little thick yesterday, about publication, during their campus tour. But then that was his job, wasn't it? She'd *better* know the lay of the land. This profession was changing. More and more, publication was the thing, even for small colleges like Midway. And it was only fair to let the new hires know up front just what the game plan was going to be. Publish or perish. Some folks cracked under that kind of pressure. Maybe just the thought of it would send her packing for California. Where she belonged.

Then he remembered the house, Faircloth Plantation, and his wife's beaming face. That house was Arden Benbow's hostage to fortune. She would never leave, he knew, of her own volition. He remembered her dark eyes inking over when he had spoken to her yesterday about being a team player. No, she would never be on his team. Not her.

He sank his whiskery, miserable face into his hands. He would be ruined. And Bobbi June right along with him.

But somehow, summoning up her image pulled into view also what might be the solution. Was his wife not forever telling him that taking everything on himself was not healthy, was in fact bad for his heart? That others needed to take some of the load of responsibility? And wasn't this the same as what the president was always saying, and the provost too, about Midway being a team? And if they were truly a team at Midway College, then maybe it was time to hand the ball off to another player.

In his fantasy he saw a thin uniformed figure weaving toward him to receive. Closer and closer the form came, until he could just make out the features. It was Booth Hazard. Booth Hazard, his lips moving almost imperceptibly inside his shadowy helmet, saying "Give us the minority line; we can use a good, talented woman."

Dean Kilgore stood up in his rumpled pajamas, lifted down the receiver from the yellow wall phone, and began dialing the English department office.

Chapter 9

Spode

Bertha Michaels, assistant chair of the English department, on this bright June morning was savoring the luxury of adding a few carefully considered puzzle pieces to Monet's "Water Lilies" spread out for the summer months on a card table close to her patio door. A cup of Earl Grey sat convenient to her left hand while the right was poised over a piece that might possibly be part of the emerging top right hand border. She had just begun her summer break, a respite she has longed for during these nine long months. And now at last she was free to coax forth her tranquil self, the one who mused over jigsaw puzzles, watched birds through binoculars, collected shells at the seaside, caught up on the latest fiction.

Yes, this was the time she spent every year replenishing herself after the terrors of two semesters with intractable youths who, if they were not from wealthy families, would certainly be classified as idiots or delinquents. They dozed through Donne, were indifferent to Crashaw, mocked Marlowe and loathed the divine Milton.

Really, what was she to do? They either could not, did not or would not read. It was partly out of this frustration that she had turned to administration. For her taste, teaching was too much like mothering.

She sighed and fit another rosy piece into the pattern. Three or four more years until retirement. She had invested some time ago in a retirement home in Del Webb's Sun City outside Palm Springs, which she now rented to responsible tenants as a tax write-off but which upon retiring she would reclaim, refurbish and settle into, spending her life observing the rare and subtle birds of the greater desert in their natural habitat. Doing as she pleased. She smiled at the thought of her own protective habitat, one from which young people—with their needs and demands and excuses—would be, by deed and by covenant, forever excluded.

Also, and here she paused with a particularly difficult puzzle piece between her thumb and forefinger, she might even perhaps live a little less for the public eye, a little more for herself. As she sat contemplating certain forbidden pleasures, the phone rang. Rising suddenly, she jostled the fragile table, and several pieces along the bottom border shook loose, as if from a tremor of the earth so slight it could not be recorded.

In her room she caught the phone on the third ring, stood by the bed nodding in agreement while Booth Hazard, her superior at the college, spoke in hushed tones of a certain extremely delicate matter that had come up requiring a woman's touch, and so quite naturally—though he was aware she had the summer off—he thought of her. Would she be so kind as to come round and see him in his office today at, say eleven?

She would.

Hazard sat behind a glowing rosewood desk of immense size backlit by a window providing a view of Midway's rugby field. Talking on the phone, he mimed an invitation for Bertha to sit, then waved his secretary in to take her request for coffee. She preferred tea, she whispered.

"Quite right," he said, momentarily holding his hand over the receiver. "Tea for two, then, Martha."

Bertha waited patiently for her tea, for their time together, watching and not watching the random patterns formed by all those dwarfed male figures running around on a green background, their diluted voices scarcely reaching the administrative offices through thick glass and the hum of central air conditioning.

Her own office was housed not in the Administration Building but instead with the rest of English. In the trenches, was how Hazard had described it to her when making the offer. With a window but no secretary. Released time (one course off) but no raise. She was to remain in the trenches, keeping an eye on things, reporting to him.

She studied him now across the expanse of desk, his starched white collar, the brown and white tie with discreet gold quill tie tack, gold cuff links just visible beneath the cuff of his beige suit jacket. His manicured fingers neatly balanced a teak and gold Montblanc pen. He gave three warning taps, a brief goodbye and looked up to greet the tray his secretary set between them.

"Sugar? Cream? Lemon?"

Accepting only a crescent of lemon, she studied the translucent Spode cup, its pink roses and gold rim. She inhaled imported Earl Grey. The chair of English neatly wrapped the string of his tea bag around the spoon and squeezed once, dropped the dry bag into his trash container and slid it under his desk out of sight.

He looked up at her with a smile, almost apologetic, boyish. "I think you know how much I rely on you, Bertha, as assistant chair of this department. Don't you? I may not always make that quite clear, as clear as I might."

"We're always so busy, Dr. Hazard. There's never really been much time for . . ."

"Exactly. Never enough time. You've put your finger on it exactly, Bertha. Of course summer's quieter, but then that's your time for a much needed rest, a little peaceful scholarship. Right, Bertha? Just you and Richard Crashaw, so to speak. But nevertheless . . . And I think you know that when the time comes . . . I do think of retirement, you know. In the not-too-distant future. Tempus fugit and all that. So yes, I do think of retirement and when I do, I can really think of no one better suited. Than you, I mean. And that's why here, up here on the battlements, in the summer, when admittedly there's less to be done, when something big comes up, something more appropriately handled, to be perfectly honest, by you, why I know I can always count on you. A woman's touch, I mean, Bertha, Miss Michaels, Dr. Michaels, rather."

Was he blushing? She told him to call her Bertha, as always, that yes, of course he could count on her, trust her to do on his behalf what he himself might, had he the time. That she had been honored by his selecting her as his assistant last summer and hoped her performance this academic year had not failed to please.

He assured her the case was quite the contrary, that if it had not been so he would hardly be approaching her now in a matter of such import. The case being that of Arden Benbow, the new minority hire. "It has come to my attention," he said, leaning close, then stopping dead. "That is to say. Certain rumors, but most of them by now substantiated. One could almost say it has to do with marching, Bertha, to the beat of a different drummer."

He glanced at his Rolex, stretched out the band as if to open the matter up for observation. "Do you follow?"

She did.

"And what I'm hoping for from you, in this extremely delicate matter, is simply to represent the best interests of this department. As only you can. In your own inimitable way, Dr. Michaels."

"But, sir . . ."

"I'm confident," he said, rising, extending his cool, soft hand, "that you will know exactly what to do. In the way of keeping an eye on things and letting me know. I'm sure you're aware that the provost is not a man who likes surprises. No more are any of us, I should think."

In four minutes she found herself driving slowly past the same rugby boys, larger now that they were up close, their beefy faces flushed and dripping perspiration. But soon they appeared only in her rearview mirror, growing smaller again. She took a deep breath, the first, perhaps, since entering the chair's office.

Beyond the boys, cows grazed, facing one direction only, as if in silent worship. Now she turned at the Midway crossroads, keeping carefully to the pavement, past Faircloth Plantation falling to ruins. Turning onto I-10, Bertha Michaels felt the larger world opening back up before her as she headed toward Tallahassee and home, where the puzzle of Monet's water lilies awaited her, spread out invitingly on the card table just as she had left it and where her field glasses and birding book rested on the chair by the glass door leading into her garden.

Home was where she felt safe. And yet as she drove toward refuge, her thoughts took a perilous detour. Stroking the wooden wheel of her Mercedes unaccountably reminded her of the attractive and costly texture of Hazard's rosewood desk and of the fine porcelain cup her superior had extended to her. She would remember always the refracted light glowing through the slender wall of the cup like the moment of trust that had passed between them.

She would see what she could do.

Chapter 10

Strictly Formal

It was a fact that Bobbi June never would understand men. Here she was, standing next to her husband at the president's ball, an event that happened once a year and in the president's own private house. Mansion, really. She knew houses and this one had cost a pretty penny, built for him by the college on the model of Thomas Jefferson's home in Monticello, except of course with plumbing and electricity. Just being here made you feel like you were part of something larger than only yourself or even your family. And besides that, it was purely wonderful to be standing here in the president's personal ballroom, where most people never got to go except twice a year—Christmas and this event tonight, the Summer Welcome for New Faculty—and instead of setting business aside and just having fun for a change, here they all were, these men, swarming like a bunch of fire ants somebody had stirred up with a big, angry stick.

Only four woman were actually dancing and one of them was

Bertha Michaels, who always dragged along that moth-eaten professor emeritus from FSU who somehow reminded Bobbi June of her daddy's mangy old stuffed owl, the way his eyes glistened behind his glasses in a flat kind of way, not following a living word you were saying. That nice Jane Oliver, gone now on sabbatical to God knew where, used to swear Bertha rented him from central casting. The other dancing men were the kind Billy Wayne called "out of the loop."

Bobbi June never could understand what loop it was and why they were out of it. Billy Wayne never could explain it to her except as a force of nature, like rain or hail.

So while those outside the loop danced and talked with women, not just men, those inside the loop did a funny kind of square dance among themselves. First the provost would stand next to the vice president and say things sideways in his ear, then up would come Strickland, from the board. Then Strickland would go off and the chair of English would come up, and then St. John the poet would come up and storm off as fast, and then whoever was left, they would all go at it until suddenly, as if somebody had given a signal, they'd all slow down, honor their partners and corners, then commence the next round, all over again.

Bobbi June had kept a firm grip on the sleeve of her Billy Wayne's tuxedo jacket so he would stand by her and even maybe dance with her once in a while. All this time she had felt him straining in the direction of the boys, like an old hound on a leash who had picked up the scent and would die if he couldn't be off and howling alongside the others in the pack.

Maybe she should just let him go. Because this seemed to be what the boys thought was fun. Like when they went off in the flat woods fooling with guns together and sleeping on the wet ground instead of in their beds next to their lawful wives where they belonged. They had always seemed like a different kind of creature from her anyway.

What she really wanted was Billy Wayne to pay some attention to her, especially tonight when she'd had her hair done and was dressed fit to kill and all on purpose. She had something to celebrate on account of getting the binder on the old Faircloth place this afternoon. That sale would push her over into the Million Dollar Club at last.

And then it hit her. All this sniffing and howling that had gone way beyond anything she had ever witnessed before was about Dr. Arden Benbow and Mr. Topaz Wilson. Her clients. She had known on that first day of house hunting there was going to be trouble, and then one thing followed along right after the next the way it always did, until she had plain forgot to be watchful and protective of her man. Her hand tightened on his sleeve.

Poor Billy Wayne. He might've been better off marrying that Winona Glass after all. Million Dollar Club or no Million Dollar Club. Billy Wayne's mama had been pulling for Winona Glass all along, even though half the county said the Glasses were nothing but trash—every last one of them—and always had been.

At the exact same moment she was fixing to ask Billy Wayne if he was ever sorry he picked her instead of Winona Glass, the provost raised his right eyebrow, and Billy Wayne suddenly broke loose and was hightailing it straight across the dance floor, dodging Bertha Michaels and the stuffed owl.

But then Bobbi June was suddenly distracted from the main swarm. Something out of the corner of her eye—for she had excellent peripheral vision—claimed her attention. A mauve apparition. Arden Benbow in a mauve tuxedo, trimmed, if Bobbi June was not mistaken, in pearl gray velvet piping with tie and matching cummerbund, the whole set off by gray patent leather opera pumps. On her arm came Mr. Topaz Wilson in a black tuxedo and looking very distinguished with a paisley gray, navy and crimson tie and cummerbund. Arden's hair was of course still sticking straight up from where she got bit by the chiggers last week, but somehow the crown of it seems soft and inviting and part of her stunning outfit itself.

Without realizing what she was doing, she moved trance-like across the dance floor toward her strange new friends.

Chapter 11
After the Ball is Over

"How did I get here?" asked Arden, lying on her bed late that night in the Dixie Court Motel, staring at the ceiling.

Topaz, flipping fitfully through the four available TV channels, paused, remote in hand. "Honey, at the stroke of midnight you flew down those stairs, same as I did. We lost our glass slippers together."

"I mean how did I get to Florida?"

"The same way I did. Very same. We hitched up the sky blue hearse to that cursed U-Haul, put her in drive and cruised across on I-10. That was it. I-10 the whole damn way! Well mostly. If you don't count the part that was just dashes on the map."

"I'm not speaking literally. I'm speaking figuratively. I just mean, what has brought me to this pass? And I'm not really asking you. I'm asking the Master of Design."

"You got to ask those questions during his shift. He's off duty and so am I. We both just want to lie here for what's left of this miserable night watching old Bette Davis movies and trying to forget that terrible party you made us go to."

"The Master of Design is not male."

Silence fell, then Bette Davis stamped her foot and said, "Philip, give me the letter!" Arden looked over at her friend and read his face. "Am I being insufferable again, Topaz? It's just that I'm lonesome, and my chigger bites itch and I hate academe with a passion. I'm in a bad mood."

"Come on over here, then, sweet thing." Topaz flung his covers back and plumped up the pillow next to him. "We'll just lie here together and eat this whole damn family size bag of potato chips until we both feel better."

"I think the dean wants me to quit. Did you see the way they all looked at me?" She settled her head onto the pillow. "Did you? Why are deans and presidents and board members so rancorous by nature? How have I offended them?"

"Here," he said, "you're not getting enough potato chips. Now watch Bette get her way. Would she let a little old dean stop her? No sir. She eats deans and provosts for lunch. Soon as your head stops itching you're going to feel so much better. Now ain't you? Here, eat your chips."

"If he makes people like me go away then there'll only be people like him left."

"That'd be a bitch. Besides, they've had it all to themselves long enough, those folks. Let's just bring along our potato chips and our tuxedos and cozy on up to them."

"It's not only the college people that are making me feel funny. Do you realize, Topaz, that we've been in Tallahassee for a week and never set eyes on one gay or lesbian person? Aren't you getting the least bit tired of straight people?"

" 'Course I am. And white people too!"

"And white people too. But you'll be gone soon. You'll be gone, and I'll be left here all alone in the South, extravagantly alienated by virtue of race, art, temperament and sexual preference."

Topaz raised himself up on one elbow. "Where did you get that tone? That's my tone. Nobody but me gets to be aggrieved. Those chigger bites are acting up on you for real."

She smiled at him.

"But seriously, you can't possibly be the only homosexual in a town the size of Tallahassee. Now Midway, that's another thing. Yeah, yeah, I know. You're going to live in Midway. That's cool. I'm just saying if ten percent of the population is gay then even in Midway there must be seven and a half of us. Your college itself has probably got three, not counting you. But Tallahassee? There's got to be five thousand here." He holds aloft a potato chip. "Think of it, five thousand beautiful but terrified people working state jobs and teaching the young. They're just hiding out until time catches up. The flower-bedecked float is coming for them.

"Haven't you noticed everything and everybody in a radius of five hundred miles is about twenty years behind the times, give or take? And that's being kind. Honest to God it feels like the fifties around here. *I Love Lucy* and *Father Knows Best* rolled into one."

"Yes," she said, staring hard at the ceiling of the Dixie Court Motel. "I even miss women. Surely to God there are some."

"Bobbi June is a woman."

Arden smiled. "Yes, Bobbi June. I like Bobbi June. Bobbi June's a woman. There must be others. I'm going out to find our people tomorrow," she said, searching the bottom of the bag for the small chips. "If they're here, I'll find them."

"You're going to *close* on your house tomorrow. That's what you're doing tomorrow."

"And then you'll be leaving."

"There's that tone again. What is it with you?"

"I'm starving," she said. "I'm just starving to death. That's all."

"The way you were going after the president's banquet tables? We could call out for a pizza if you're serious. An all-night pizzeria. I guess they have that here."

"I'm starving for my own food. Do you realize how long it's been since we had a taco or an enchilada?"

"Texas?"

"Yes, Texas. You don't know what it's like, trying to live without Mexican food. I lived in Iowa for three years while Malthus worked on his degree. Three years. I even tried canned tortillas! Old El Paso canned tortillas. They smelled and tasted exactly like cork. What am I going to do here?"

"This is not Iowa. There are folks in Florida for whom tortillas are staples."

"Cubans don't eat tortillas. I'm here alone without my people or my language or my culture."

"And I'm chopped liver?"

"You're leaving me. You're going to the land of combination plates and mariachis."

"I'll mail you some masa. Really, I promise. Now let's get some shut-eye. Like I said, you're closing tomorrow. Your *bidness* mind needs its beauty sleep."

"Why do they call it a 'closing'? What a mournful word. Poe would have liked it better than *nevermore* if he'd thought of it."

"Yeah," he said, "I know what you mean. Closing. Sounds like the gate to your cell swinging shut behind you. I guess like birth, marriage and death, buying a house is a deed not easily undone. I hold my breath for you."

"Have you ever wanted a house of your own, Tope?"

"Not me. Tom, though, I think he's drawn to closings and openings and such. You know, all the markers of domesticity and general lifelong changelessness."

Arden sighed, wadding up the empty potato chip bag and arcing it into the trashcan. "Maybe that's what scares me. The permanence of it."

"Nothing's permanent, Chicken Little. Except maybe those mortgage payments you're signing up for. God knows the house itself is going to crumble away underneath you quick enough. Just promise me two things."

"Two things?"

"Just two. One, you ain't goin' to buy you no lawn mower, and two, you ain't never going to sell your Harley. Just wait till that dean sees you on your fine motorcycle!"

"I promise," she said, kissing his cheek and tumbling into her own bed.

"Good," said Topaz in a voice like satin, as he turned out the light. "That's good. You be fine."

Chapter 12
Closing/Opening

When Arden arrived at the Midway College Credit Union, Lamar Littleton, senior loan officer, was just finishing his nonfat cherry yogurt.

"Are we not to have the pleasure of Mr. Wilson's company then?" Mr. Littleton asked.

"Mr. Wilson sends his regrets." Momentarily she considered the possibility of having some of her own. But no, she was sure. La Malinche, requiring permanence and stability, urged her forward. Time seconded the motion. She would close, as scheduled.

Mr. Littleton led her down the hall. The pale blue carpets and matching walls smelled like the inside of a new refrigerator. Arden followed him into a conference room with a long empty table and ballpoint pens set carefully before each of four chairs. It looked a little like the room where she defended her dissertation. So many chairs and pens, so little air. Her face flushed and her chigger bites began to itch.

Just then Bobbi June bustled in, kissing Arden's flushed cheek and squeezing her shoulder for reassurance, then sat down on her right, filling the empty air with perfume, apology and confidence. She had done this hundreds of times, this good woman. It would be all right.

Next, a short man with a glittering bald head arrived, Mr. Stony Burke, attorney for Mr. Giles Gifford, longtime absentee owner. Mr. Burke shook hands all around, sat down and began alternately burrowing in his brief case then patting the little pockets in his vest, as if he had lost something of inestimable value.

Mr. Littleton waited a moment, then apparently deciding that Mr. Burke's searches were nothing more than a nervous habit, launched into a monologue explaining to Arden the first of a dozen legal-sized sheets bearing fine print. He stopped and gestured with his pen at certain key passages, like a flight attendant explaining the use of oxygen devices and flotation cushions in the unlikely event of an emergency.

Arden pretended to listen. Sometimes, she had observed, in order to get one's way, one must first allow those in charge to exhaust themselves. She was willing. She was patient. She pretended to read over the documents as he handed them to her, each in its turn. Whenever Bobbi June nodded, Arden signed next to the x that Mr. Littleton had made with his fat ballpoint pen.

She did not understand half of it. Nobody did these days, Bobbi June had warned her. She *did* know, however, that she was borrowing an extra $15,000 for renovations and that the college itself was to hold this mortgage with its extremely generous interest rate as a courtesy to new faculty.

But something in the sea of small fonts caught her eye. She had a glimmer of recognition over clause iii-b of p. 13 of the seventh document. It said, "Buyer affirms that no portion of the down payment has been borrowed." Strictly speaking, Arden understood that the cashier's check she had obtained with a cash advance from Visa did mean borrowing. She also understood if she did not initial the clause, then she would not get the plantation on which her pastoral future depended.

Was she not a poet, one who understood truth in metaphoric and symbolic terms? "Bust your cards," Topaz had said, quoting the lifelong advice of his Aunt Hazel. Therefore, next to the x, Mr. Littleton's ballpoint pen had made exactly at clause iii-b, Arden Benbow carefully inscribed a large and ornate *AB*.

Two hours later she was comfortably seated in what Mr. Littleton was pleased to call "the alternative bookstore." Several alternative people roamed the shop, and an obliging salesperson named Lisa had provided Arden with a cup of coffee, the latest Adrienne Rich and an intriguing book by a local lesbian scholar who several years ago had retreated into the mountains of North Carolina to raise llamas. Lisa personally found the book dry and academic, but many of the alternative clientele had loved it. Arden flipped it open to page three:

Each of us is a heroine in our own novel of manners. We enter an alien society whose ways we can neither comprehend nor admire. Our survival depends on our understanding that the rules held out to us as social outsiders or even outlaws are not synonymous with the power principles by which the organism actually operates.

In other words, the rules society deliberately recommends to the alien or entering person are not the rules that actually prevail. Therefore the entering person must not depend on society itself for effective teaching. Indeed, society desires only that the entrant comply with the code of behavior, not that s/he becomes sufficiently knowledgeable to claim a share in the mechanisms of power.

Arden had stopped breathing. She must have this book. Ostensibly a dry treatise on the novel of manners, it was really a conduct manual for lesbian academics.

She leapt to her feet, momentarily disoriented in the store. Reading sometimes had this effect on her, disturbed her equilibrium so that now she rose from her chair reeling, staggering. At last she made her way to the cash register and to the amused Lisa.

For the second time in a single day Arden Benbow's Visa card saved her life.

Chapter 13
Blueprint

At the very moment Topaz kicked open the front door, staggering under the weight of a huge box labeled "Hillary's Room," a brittle-winged creature in burnished armor flew straight for his face. He threw down the box and flung himself onto the floor, all six-three of him.

A man with a gray ponytail just behind him laughed. "Welcome to Florida," he said. "That's one of them flying roaches."

"Is there another kind, Butch?" Topaz asked from the floor. "Not funny, Arden." He got to his feet and dusted off his jeans. "Nature's getting the upper hand here. Have you done anything yet about the fleas in the parlor?"

"You got fleas in your parlor?" Butch guffawed.

"Listen, Butch," said Arden, "if you're going to work with me, you're going to have to control yourself a little. Not much, but a little."

"Lips, don't unpurse," said Butch with equanimity.

"Arden, which room is Hillary's?" Topaz had shouldered the box once again.

"Attic, west side, Tope. Now Butch, let's go into the kitchen." She spread out on the kitchen counter three sheets of drafting paper numbered one through three, a separate sheet for each floor. "Butch, the first and most important thing you've got to do is make the house tight and livable."

"Yes 'um, and that means roof, windows and replacing siding. You got bad wood rot. I hate to say it." He beamed.

"Whatever it takes. And I want insulation in the attic. The best you can find."

"Right."

"Next comes Operation Bathroom. It goes here," she said, tapping her red pen on page one, "in what is now the sewing room. And make sure all the other plumbing works. We've got six kids. Now can you do all this work yourself? Bobbi June says you're the best in Midway."

"If I can't do it, I got a cousin or two as can. So you're covered, all except for the sheetrock. And it takes a certain personality to make a good sheetrock man. But I think I can lay my hands on one, time we get goin' on the bathroom. Y'all wantin' to live here while this is going on? I don't recommend it, for both our sakes."

"It'll be just me in that upstairs front bedroom."

"Suit yourself." Butch rolled up the drawings. "Now Jimmy Freebeau, he tells me he's doing the AC, so him and me will work out the timing. He's a good man. Oh, and just one more thing, ma'am." Suddenly Butch looked embarrassed. "They're sayin' down to the post office and the Unocal that you folks are . . . well, that y'all . . . are different. *Real* different. If you take my meaning. Ma'am."

"I do, Butch," said Arden. "I take your meaning perfectly. My primary relationship is with a woman, Alice, whom you'll eventually meet. She is a woman of sense and sensibility. I think, too, that I exhibit those same qualities in preferring her company to that of a man. So while you say I am different—a judgment I embrace—in a way you and I are just alike."

"Ma'am?"

"I take it you do prefer women, Butch."

"Oh, yes ma'am, God love 'em."

"Then we are not so far apart after all, Butch."

"I guess. I mean, I hope you don't take no offense, me asking and all. On account of what they're saying."

"Down to the Unocal."

"Yes 'um. And me, I just like to kind of know where I'm at, get the lay of the land and all, up front."

"Butch, I suspect everybody wants to know the lay of the land."

"Even you, from time to time," said Topaz appearing in the doorway. "Even you."

"Especially me," she laughed. "Now Butch, can we get back to—"

"Yes ma'am we can," he said, taking the blueprints. "I'll just go see where Jimmy Freebeau has got to."

"Labor problems?" asked Topaz when they are alone.

"Just a little xenophobia. Got a minute? There's something I want to show you. Something to do with the lay of the land."

She led him upstairs and into the front bedroom. Topaz turned around slowly. "What are we doing here in Hillary's room?"

"It's yours, if you want it. And the strange bathroom too. Private. With a lock on the door."

"I don't know, Arden," he said, collapsing onto the window seat. "This is a sweet room, but it's Hill's. She's Emily Bronte, not me. This whole South thing. I know I told you that Florida wasn't the South, but it turns out it is after all. Besides, Tom's waiting."

"Yes, I know," she said, sinking down next to him on the window seat. "There *is* Tom. And how could I not want for you what I have with Alice? But I am going to miss you so. It was wonderful of you to come so far."

"I worry about you, sweet thing," he said stroking her hand. "You going to be okay in this crazy place?"

"Not so crazy."

"Crazy. Think about it. What's the first thing that happened to me this morning? The flying roaches. Now answer me this. What other vermin have imperiled your life since you got here? Forgive me if I mention the small matter of the chiggers. Then of course we have the fleas, if I'm not mistaken, which first appeared on your ankles and have since set up serious housekeeping in the parlor. You're the one who tends to think symbolically. Not me."

"I give up. I do note that we have a trinity of vermin, if that's your point. Am I missing something? What in your mind do the chiggers, fleas and roaches symbolize?"

"You're losing your imagination or your sense of humor, one. Now think." He waited. "Oh hell. Deans, provosts and vice presidents is what. The insect world directly correlates with the academic world. It's scary. I tell you, Arden, I'm afraid to leave you here alone."

"Alone?" she said.

They sat in silence for a moment. Then, as if on cue, they heard the roll of distant thunder, joined in a moment by Butch's crowbar ripping away siding from the porch and Jimmy Freebeau's hammer chiming in the attic. They looked at each other and laughed. When it seemed nothing else could possibly increase the din, they heard an engine roaring and backfiring. From their perch on the window seat they turned together to look down onto the scene.

An ancient Chrysler of uncertain color and vintage approached, slowed at the crossroads, then turned onto the hard road and stopped, its engine idling raggedly. An elderly black woman eased herself out of the passenger seat, straightened, said a few words to the driver, then drew out a heavy shopping bag and after that her cane. Hattie White began her customary journey along the footpath that crossed Arden's land, balancing the weight of her provisions, toward home.

Chapter 14
The Third Thing

Arden stood at the airport window until she saw Topaz's plane taxi down the runway and lift off into the night. Then she exited the building in a flurry of moths and steam. The parking lot was deserted, silent. The hearse sat alone like a huge, dark fish. Above, the sliver of a moon shimmered through cobwebs of mist. "Florida," she whispered, as to a lover, and unlocked the door.

She liked the feel of being enclosed all cocoon-like inside, the air conditioning clicking on and off like a life support system as she turned onto the highway and the smooth, cushioned ride.

When she left the highway, following what Bobbi June called the "hard road" into Midway, she glided past the silent buildings of the campus where a few students passed like shadows down the softly lighted walks. Who were they? How would she teach them?

Along the eastern boundary, sleeping cows stood in patterns across the landscape like ancient stones set down long ago by alien peoples.

At the crossroads, the hard road gave out, and Arden rocked along the two-rut road toward her own land where she would spend her first night alone, under the moon of new beginnings.

She parked the car, slammed the door and started up the porch stairs, feeling for the loose board with her toe. Maybe Butch had been right about putting in a floodlight. What was it he had said? That nights out here could get "dark as Egypt," and was Egypt dark? She stopped, contemplating the question, when she became aware of a sound, a pulsating sound, as if her own heart had somehow become a piece of farm machinery.

What could it be, and wasn't the country supposed to be quiet?

Then she remembered Bobbi June had warned her, told her as she told all her "Yankee" customers settling down in the country for the first time, that "frogs can make enough ruckus to scare you half to death till you get used to it like I am." One new resident on the first night in his new house had called the sheriff.

Fortified by the recollection, Arden opened the front door—no need to lock anything, Bobbi June had assured her—and groped around for the light switch, flipped it. And . . . no lights. They had promised her. Not for nothing were they called the power company. Some damn renegade co-op of a power company. One day she would make her own electricity, she swore. In the meantime she had a flashlight in her glove compartment.

Armed now with light, she followed the narrow beam back up the stairs, spied something just left of the door, a bottle tied up with cascades of pink and aluminum ribbon, leaning against the wall like a small, festive drunk. The luminous gift tag she held under the flashlight beam read: "Congratulations to you, Arden honey, new mistress of Faircloth Plantation."

She carried the bottle into the house, and stood in the giant hall, breathing in the scent of a century of striving, the antique smells of daily life. The bottle felt cool in her hand, but her eyes saw only shapes, as if she had somehow wandered into the belly of time.

Was she afraid? No. She was home at last. Carrying the champagne like a chalice, she walked down the hall into the kitchen and set it on the sloping counter. Major work needed to be done in the kitchen. She dug through boxes, searching for a wine glass, any glass, settled for a large Pyrex measuring cup.

She climbed the stairs to the mistress suite, where she had made up a single mattress on the floor. Monkish but cozy. In the big strange bathroom she performed her ablutions by flashlight then changed into her pajamas. Out of the corner of her eye she detected something moving along the baseboard. Momentarily she saw a small black shape in the beam of light, a skittering something. She thought of Topaz and his admonitions, his worry, his advice. His love.

She would be fine. This was not a time of loneliness and terrors but rather a time of solitary jubilation.

Pajama-clad, she carried the champagne onto the balcony, eased out the cork with her thumbs, poured the measuring cup full, lifted it. She would toast her new house. But could she continue to call it Faircloth Plantation? Surely not. Instead she claimed this place now in the name of all the dispossessed, this home which would henceforth be known as . . . be known as . . . Crossroads Gardens.

True, she thought, pouring herself another measuring cup of Bobbi June's champagne, there were as yet no gardens. But that was a technicality. Closing her eyes she saw row upon row of raised garden plots, holding unknown plants with thick green leaves. Leaves to feed the world. She lifted her measuring cup in a toast to Crossroads Gardens. She trickled a little bubbly over the balcony for Tonantzín, and then— just in case—a little for Coatlicue. She stood a while, listening to the thrumming of the crickets, the *basso continuo* of the bullfrogs, watching little winking lanterns of passing fireflies, contemplated, then hummed, sang a little. Had another half cup champagne. Considered how nice it was of Bobbi June to leave a gift, imagined her running open scissors over the ribbon, shaping the curls in tribute and friendship.

She was not sleepy. Where was that book she bought the other day? In graduate school, literary criticism had never failed to put her to sleep. She snuggled into her bed, her head on two pillows, the flashlight resting on her breastbone, and reached for the ultimate soporific. Outside the windows sound rose and fell, rose and fell, rose and fell like the very breath of night. She opened the book.

Arden liked to start in the middle, read to the end, and then conclude with the beginning. When a line jumped out at her, there would she start. This one said: *The heroine resides in the zone created by tensions existing between the demands of society and the requirements of self.* Critics certainly used a lot of prepositions, and this one was no exception. What could the poor woman be trying to say?

But she would read on. She sipped more champagne and plumped up her pillows, adjusted the flashlight on her chest. Next, her eye fell on the line, *Innocence must become educated.* Now she was really getting irritated. She had always considered innocence an enlightened response to what passed for evil in the world. Innocence was not, after all, synonymous with stupidity, notwithstanding her ex-husband's opinion on that subject.

Here the flashlight rolled off her chest and clattered to the floor. She had hoped for a restful transition into the dreamtime and instead she was arguing with Malthus, who was, mercifully enough, more than three thousand miles away.

She flipped to the opening chapter. Now this was very interesting. Apparently in a novel of manners the heroine characteristically appeared at a ball where she attracted much notice. Arden rested the book on her stomach while her mind drifted back to the president's Summer Welcome for New Faculty and the feel of a thousand eyes on her cropped hair and mauve tuxedo. Academic xenophobia, it seemed, was as real as its rural counterpart. She would see what else the book had to say.

Unlike the hair of the picaro, which is often cut short in a ritual of initiation (see Smollett's Roderick Random), *the soft curls of the heroine of manners remain untouched, emphasizing both her innocence and her vulnerability (See Austen's* Pride and Prejudice).

Which was she, then? Roderick Random or Elizabeth Bennett? Or possibly she was some third thing, a *picara* trapped in a world of unfamiliar and unintelligible manners.

She poured herself another quarter cup of champagne. Perhaps moving to the South meant she must inevitably segue from *picara* to ingenue. Transformation, it seemed, was not for the faint of heart. Nor for the weary either, and she was weary. For the time being, she would simply finish her cup of champagne and go quietly to sleep.

But when she began to drift off, she saw herself standing in the doorway of the president's ballroom wearing her mauve tuxedo, being ogled across the room by Mr. Darcy who turned from her in disgust. He whispered into the ear of his comrade, Mr. Bingley, and somehow she could hear every word. "This lady," Darcy informed his friend in impeccable BBC English, "will never, ever be awarded tenure by me."

"Or anyone else, for that matter," Arden added softly, turning off her flashlight.

Chapter 15

East of Sumatra

Drip, drip, drip. Arden woke to what sounded like the opening paragraph of *Bleak House*. Drip, drip, dripping, not all over London, but onto her chest, precisely where last night she had lodged the flashlight.

Then there came a bang, bang, banging on the front door. She leapt up and stepped out onto the balcony. Below her at the front door stood Butch in a black poncho, rain dripping off the bill of his ball cap as he gazed up at his new employer in her pink pajamas.

"Morning, ma'am," he said, touching his cap. "Sorry to wake you up. But me and Sammy Two's here to get started on that roof of yours, soon as this lets up. Oughtn't to last long."

"It's time I was up anyway, Butch," she shouted over the railing. "Wish I could stay and help, but I'm going job hunting today."

"I'd rather fix the roof, ma'am. I'd rather have the toothache. Bad enough job hunting, but things in Tallahassee are tight as a tick. Either there ain't no job or it's going to the boss's cousin, never mind you seen it in the papers and you can do the work. Like they say, it ain't what you know, it's who. And you don't know nobody."

"Butch, honey," she called down gaily, "that remains to be seen."

An hour later Arden pulled up under an oak, running the air conditioning, and searching on her map for Sumatra, then County Road 7. Sumatra. She liked the sound of it. Fevered dreams of the tropics threatened to overwhelm her, divert her from her mission.

For she had been following meticulously the directions to Full Court Press given her last week at the bookstore by the young woman. Lisa had told her that the lesbian press usually hired during the summer months. And Arden, as both householder and mother of six, needed something to tide her over until the fall semester began. It was worth a try.

The rain had let up, and the sun struggled for the upper hand. Clearly she was in territory Butch fondly referred to as East Jesus. Mostly rolling hills, some of it cultivated, some of it enshrouded in kudzu, waiting to be discovered by those who, like Bobbi June, were bent on making a living by selling Florida.

Finally, eureka, Arden found herself on the map. In an eighth of an inch more she'd run into County Road 7. She eased the hearse back onto the road and soon passed a country church with a battered electric sign saying in red plastic letters, "Fearing God is the beginning of wisdom." On the opposite side of the road, another sign, this one professionally lettered on wood, said FULL COURT PRESS AND WRITERS RETREAT. PRIVATE PROPERTY. POSTED.

She turned right onto the retreat's two-rut road. POSTED. Must be something to do with the postal system. These strange codes and customs and assumptions. If she only had a map to these, a guide to the South that identified and translated signs, gestures, glyphs, tropes, metaphors and other curious habits of being. She felt like a blind creature set down in a strange world.

Through the pines she spotted a cedar house of some size and generous appointments, then to the left a barn with lots of cars and trucks in front. A couple of burly young women loaded boxes into a truck bed. A cat lounged on the roof of the cab, its tail hanging down in the rear window like a pendulum.

"Wow, fine car!" said one of the baby dykes approaching her window even before Arden could turn off the ignition. "You one of the writers?"

"Well, I am a poet," said Arden, getting out and taking the welcoming hand of the second baby dyke.

"Must not be one of Granny's writers. Boss Granny hasn't got much use for poets."

"No, I'm not one of her writers, but I would like to see her about a job. A menial job. I'm humble."

"Humble is a strong recommendation around here. Come on in."

Arden followed her into the barn—the insides looked like a combination warehouse and office suite. Books were stacked everywhere, and women at a counter packed boxes, loading them onto UPS carts. It seemed like a Santa's village of books sequestered in the nowhere east of Sumatra.

The young woman opened a door and directed her into a carpeted hall. "Just go on down there and announce yourself. She's in the last office on your right."

Arden nodded and quietly moved down the hall. When she reached the last office, a woman who looked for all the world like a graying baby glanced up suddenly from her desk and, fixing Arden with penetrating blue eyes, said, "Who the hell are you?"

Startled, Arden exclaimed, "A poet!"

"Another damned poet?" Boss Granny studied her through thick glasses. "Can't use you. Poetry doesn't sell. Never has, never will. Can't even *give* the damned stuff away, and believe me, I've tried. Now write me a good lesbian detective novel and we can talk turkey." She turned back to her work.

"Actually I was wondering . . . they told me at the bookstore, that you sometimes hire—"

"I do need a good gardener right now though. Can you follow orders?"

Arden laughed. "People tell me it's not my strongest suit."

Granny whooped. "Me either. I like you," she said. "You're hired. Minimum wage, mind you. Half time, and you'll want to make that half in the mornings. Goddamn heat'll kill you, if I don't. Let's go on the tour, and then I've got work to do, my poet friend." She got to her feet and led the way into a kitchen. "You poets are so damned moony-eyed. Hope you can keep your wits about you. Last gardener we had didn't know a weed from an orchid. Cut down ten pecan saplings in as many minutes. Fired her ass. Mind you don't pull any damn fool tricks like that. What did you say your name was?"

"Arden."

"Well Arden, you're welcome to make coffee or tea here or store your lunch in the fridge. You already saw the shipping room. That's where you came in. I've got two full-time people under me. I pay them good wages and good benefits. I like loyalty, Arden, and I'm willing to pay for it.

"I've also got twelve part-timers working with no benefits whatsoever except the valuable experience of working with a woman who's a legend in her own time and who's doing the work of the goddess and making it pay handsomely. I hope you have no objection to a successful business because that's what this is." She flung a door open and said, "Bathroom. No mystery there," then she continued on down the hall.

"The reason this business is successful is that I work night and day and so do all the people under me. The other reason it's successful is I have a clear market in mind, the large, voracious market of lesbians out there wanting to read about themselves, who aren't particularly educated but know what they like and don't mind spending their money to get it. Why shouldn't people like that be able to buy the kind of books they want?"

"So really," said Arden, studying her milky blue eyes in the dim light of the hall, "really you're an idealist."

Granny whooped again, then suddenly looked serious. "Honey, you're the first person to say so, ever. Let's go outside." The back door opened onto acres of woods with winding walks and flowerbeds and even a fledgling vineyard in the distance. The property included the cedar house and up close to that a free-form swimming pool, a cabana and a tennis court. Boss Granny defined her space with sweeps of her arm, as they strolled together down a pathway strewn with pine straw.

"They don't mess with me in Sumatra because I help prop up their sorry ass little town. I'm the greatest single user of UPS. I donate to the library, such as it is, and I employ construction workers, plumbers, electricians, you name it, all local. When Boss Granny roars, Sumatra listens."

In a moment Arden thought she saw—yes, she did—a golf ball resting on mowed grass.

"That's my golf course. Miniature, but there's nine holes, and it's a world of fun, but I never get to play any because I'm working night and day to keep this operation afloat. Some of the writers like it, though. And if they're happy, I'm happy.

"See, that's Wollstonecraft Cottage right next to the dogwood. Young woman in there writing lesbian sci fi. Very popular. She's one who almost makes a living at writing. Beyond that one's Shelley Cottage.

"I've got four more cottages scattered over my land. That's six authors altogether, pumping it out night and day. My market reads like it's going out of style, and I've got to keep up with them. Building this retreat was kind of a divine accident, you could say. I built it for a proud beauty named Sahara three years ago." Boss Granny shook her head in painful recollection. "Romance writer. Three kids and no time to write. I knew she could do it if she didn't have to work her damn day job for the state or jump around after those kids. So I built this place where she could get away and write. Writers are like that, you know. Writing is who they are. It's like air to them."

Granny paused and stared through a break in the canopy of trees. "If you love someone I guess you have got to love what they love. A damn loss that woman was. I gave her everything. Say, what's your marital status, anyway?"

"Married, with children," said Arden.

"Well I don't stoop to bird dogging another woman's woman. I respect marriage and all that. Too damn bad though. I would have been married myself, but Sahara ran off with a damn Sufi dancer came through Tallahassee one summer. Eight Days of Dance. You might have heard of it over at the university, the real one. On the sixth day of the Eight Days of Dance, my Sahara left with their lead dancer. So much for culture and religion.

"Can't say I regret building the retreat, though. It's the best little tax write-off I ever had. This part of the operation's purely nonprofit, right on down to the golf course. And then, too, I got the six writers like six geese sitting on their little nests. And believe you me, Arden, one of them, one day, is going to lay Boss Granny the golden egg. Say, you sure you couldn't write fiction?"

"I've always just written poetry. I don't think I could write genre fiction."

"That's what sells. No damn use writing anything else. Erotica, romance, detective novels, science fiction."

She stopped in front of a large shed with a tin roof. "My fiction writers work in cottages with velvet upholstered window seats, leaded glass and Jacuzzi hot tubs. Now this is where the poets work." She flings open the door, revealing a small red tractor with cart, rakes, pruning shears, shovels, sacks of fertilizer, manure and shelves of lethal brown bottles with peeling labels.

"Talk to Oak. She'll get you started. The one in the tie-dyed undershirt. I don't name them, dress them or even like them. I just employ them. Speaking of which, what in Christ's name happened to your hair?"

"Red bug," said Arden.

"You damn poets," said Boss Granny, shaking her head. "I got to get back to work. Any questions?"

"When I came in I passed a sign that said posted. What does posted mean?"

"Posted means if you're on my property, then I can damn well shoot you dead, no questions asked. That's the South for you. Don't you just love it!" Boss Granny gave one last whoop and led Arden back to the barn for a horticultural briefing by Oak.

Chapter 16
Tenure Track

The next Sunday morning Arden lay dreaming on her makeshift bed, sun playing across her left cheek. Although she didn't write narratives, she did tend to dream them, often with title and sometimes screen credits. This one was called *Ambiguities of Space: A Detective Dream*, a genre dream combining features of science fiction and detective fiction. In the first scene she was riding in the back of a paddy wagon with a green man. The guards had shackled their ankles. Then unaccountably she was rushing along inside a silver tube which dumped her out onto a familiar set. She was Starship Commander Benbow, viewing the green man on a giant screen. Her task was to free the green man from his captors. She pushed a button on the dashboard of her spacecraft and set off a terrible explosion in the paddy wagon. Quickly she glanced into the rearview mirror of her spacecraft, not to see behind but to study her own face, half of which she now saw had turned green. This seemed important. She would now beam the green man aboard. But something had gone wrong with her transporter.

She stirred on her mattress, aware of the heat on her cheek and the malfunctioning of her equipment, which now made a terrible sound like a thrown rod or a weapon someone was firing off in the command module. But surely a stunner made no noise.

She sat up, heart pounding, leaped out of bed, strode out onto the balcony and looked down the long and irregular side of her house. A woodpecker was giving her house what for, as if it were a rotten tree. "Get away," she yelled. "This is *my* house, goddamn it, not yours! And this is Sunday. My Sunday morning!"

At precisely that moment the phone rang.

She didn't even know she had a telephone. She staggered down the hall, glancing in each room, then stumbled sleepily up the stairs. Finally, under Jamie's dormer window she spied a familiar aquamarine princess phone, bearing a note in Topaz's hand: "Greetings! You are now connected to the outside world. Such as it is. Consider this a hostess gift. Topaz." She sank onto the floor, cradling the receiver. Topaz.

The world she was connected to was that of Bertha Michaels, assistant chair. Like Charles Dickens, Arden enjoyed equating people with furniture. Even at this hour the thought made her smile. Perhaps one day she herself might aspire to being a chair or table or couch. Bertha was apologizing for not having called sooner, right after the president's ball in fact. But she had been down with such a vicious head cold, and she hoped she hadn't called too early in the day but had wanted to catch Arden before she went to church.

Fear is the beginning of wisdom, thought Arden.

And how would Arden like to join her on a little excursion to St. George Island today, then a seafood supper in the quaint fishing village of Apalachicola? A little get-acquainted adventure, just the two of them.

Arden yawned, stretched out her back, which had begun to complain of yesterday's rigors in Boss Granny's east forty, and said she would be delighted.

Shortly after one, Arden was gliding through the gently rolling hills of Tallahassee's Piedmont neighborhood. Large single-story brick houses reclined under sheltering oaks on well-cut lawns fringed by vigorous beds of ivy. Arden turned into the azalea-edged drive of Professor Michaels and parked her hearse next to a Mercedes sedan of recent vintage and dark ruby hue, the second such vehicle she'd seen in as many weeks. Did Midway maintain a fleet of them?

Professor Gridley at UCLA had tried one last time to tutor her in the ways of academe before she left for Florida. Money, she had explained, though there wasn't much of it in academe, nevertheless remained very much the script of choice in this world, with prestige, whether academic or administrative, a close second. She, Arden, was not to persist in thinking of academe as a haven for idealists and lovers of literature. Here Gridley had lowered her amber-tinged eyelids and lapsing into her Tennessee drawl had said, "While, Miss Benbow, belles-lettres may have first seduced these people to the side of higher education, believe me her disreputable first cousins, lucre and security, keep them all faithful."

Bertha, like Dean Billy Wayne Kilgore, must be a high roller in the low-stakes game of academe. And there stood Bertha now, in shade and shafts of light on a mossy brick path leading to her front door, waiting for Arden. "Mind you don't slip," she said.

Arden wondered momentarily if her words meant more than they seemed, then dismissed the notion. The eyes that greeted hers were clear and gray. At Bertha's invitation, she stepped into the living room. And into another world. The American Southwest, to be exact. A huge Native American stove filled the room with its graceful, curving whiteness, like a plump, beautiful and possibly naked woman. So large was this stove that the few pieces of furniture looked like startled hostages. The whole effect was as though Bertha Michaels had installed an entire hogan inside her northwest Florida ranch style house.

"Surprised?" she asked, laying her hand tenderly against the white surface. "It's called a *kiva* fireplace. I fell helplessly in love with desert cultures during my last sabbatical."

"Love is like that," said Arden, tracing the curve with her fingers. "In fact, it's *exactly* like that. A large, warm, beautiful and apparently useless something you carry around inside your heart."

"And you can't explain it to anybody."

"No," Arden agreed. "It's beyond language. Far beyond."

As if they had gone too far too fast, Bertha said, suddenly looking distracted, off-balance, "Maybe we should be going."

"Good," said Arden, "my hearse or yours?"

As she drove toward the coast, Bertha mused, trying to muster the ragtag army her mind had become. Lately, it seemed, she could not keep it disciplined. If her colleagues had become aware of these little flights from order—had they begun with menopause?—she would never have been entrusted with the responsibility, not to mention the honor, of being named second-in-command. Strategy and discipline, she reminded her troops, who today had been routed at the first engagement with the enemy, if that's what Arden Benbow was. Certainly she was the fortress to be taken.

But assault would never work here, and that was why she, Bertha Michaels, had been called in. "A woman's touch," was how Booth had put it to her again, when he had called to remind her of their little agreement. Certainly he had been understanding about the cold she had come down with almost immediately after their first talk. But the situation had grown critical, and so she must delay no longer. He hinted obliquely that the vice president himself might have some interest in this matter. In closing he had reminded her of his confidence in her, his conviction that he might count on her, as ever.

She would not let him down. She would crawl forth under heavy fire and lash down this loose cannon that was Arden Benbow.

She glanced over at her young colleague in the passenger seat, the strong line of the jaw, the nose a trifle too large but balanced, overall by what Bertha felt tempted to call Indian features. There was a certain innocence about the full mouth, her lashes so full and dark they could be seen even at this distance. Her thick, cropped hair barely stirred in the breeze coming in at the top of the window.

Bertha drove on, while the sun and the hum of the engine and the profile of this handsome woman accented against the brilliant Gulf and the talk of love that one carried inside oneself all conspired to pull her back into another part of her life, one she kept always behind a door closed even against herself.

She had been young, oh my how young. Barely twenty-five. A raw recruit with a tenure track position at the University of Michigan. After only a year of regular service, they had sent her on their Italian Study Abroad Program, put her in charge of twenty young women perilously close to her own age and assigned her a class in the American Expatriates and another in the European Novel.

They had been thrown together, all of them, and isolated from their own culture. Expatriates themselves, they had formed an extraordinary bond. From the first, though, there had been a particular young woman, one livelier, more intelligent, quicker to appreciate, to understand. Bertha had found herself studying her eyes at dinner, her lips, the toss of her head. She struggled against her feelings and, failing that, she struggled against expression, until one day, after a long and splendid weekend in Venice, she had foolishly set pen to paper. To tell what was in her heart.

Her face burned with shame even now to think of it, more than thirty years later. The girl, confused, troubled, had written not back to her, but to her parents. Who had immediately called the director of the Italian Abroad Program, who had called the dean of students, who had called the provost, who had called her chair, who had called her up long distance to quip about her "*Death in Venice* episode" and to tell her, as he put it, "to start shopping for another job."

For two years she had to live among colleagues who knew, who whispered in the halls, who unleashed their wit on the bones of her life but who would say nothing to the outside world, their silence secure, so that in time they might be rid of her once and for all.

Finally, as if by some miracle, Midway College had offered her a haven, a second chance. She had learned to live quietly, stolidly, discreetly, had learned to serve and to exceed all standards. She had knowledge to pass on. A place. Bertha Michaels felt gratitude.

~

Later in the day—having walked down the shore as the tide drew seaward, having observed shadows of wild sea oats cast onto the curve of sand dunes and the seabirds' quick-beaked jabs toward delicacies—the two women sat at a picnic table on a deck overlooking the Apalachicola River. Arden, wearing a Boss Oysters paper bib, struggled to open a blue crab. Her hair stood up from wind and salt air. She might be fourteen, Bertha observed.

"Like this," she instructed her charge, inserting a fork between twin breast plates and pulling back the resistant flap, exposing succulent white meat. "We'll come back in September when it's safe to eat the raw oysters." Meanwhile they had broiled ones, and fish dip and smoked mullet, coleslaw and beer.

Arden looked up from her crab, sleeves rolled up, butter running down her forearms and thanked her new colleague.

Bertha cleaned her hands and slid the paper plates down to the end of the table for the waitress to pick up. She sipped her beer. The sun was sinking behind them, etching the water in rippling shades of pink. In a light almost Venetian, a fishing boat encircled by gulls chugged past them upriver. "I want to mentor you, Arden," she said, startling herself. "Professionally, I mean."

Arden raised her eyebrows quizzically, then returned to digging smoked mullet off bones with a plastic fork, watching with amusement the cats balancing on the railings waiting for diners to toss them morsels, lifting her head at the sound of screaming gulls.

Bertha, feeling strangely inspired, began. Like a sergeant briefing her chief scout before a dangerous mission, she unfolded her information, talking on and on through two more crabs and a second order of fish dip.

Finally, over coffee, she divulged her theory about the single-author career. "Find one author you can live with and then mine his or her works for your entire life. When one branch gives out, open another off the main shaft. It's not a bad life, believe me. It has its rewards. Richard Crashaw and I have made a very nice life together, I can assure you."

Arden, for the past ten minutes, had been writing feverishly on paper napkins, held down against the wind by a saltshaker and a bottle of cocktail sauce.

"Taking notes?" Bertha inquired of her protégée.

"Poems. I'm writing poems," said Arden.

"Oh well," said Bertha, "I suppose after all you are in Creative Writing."

"I'm a poet," said Arden, pen flying.

"Well then, my dear, that may be what you have to publish after all. But I do think you should shore that kind of thing up with some good solid scholarly writing, just to be on the safe side, which, believe me, is the side you want to be on.

"Shall we be getting back, then?"

Bertha set down her glimmering new American Express Card, a recent perquisite of Midway College, next to the grease-streaked bill. "My treat," she said. "I asked you." While the waitress took the card, Bertha gathered up the sheaf of text-covered napkins, carefully folded it, and handed it to Arden. And as she did, a sudden cry of a gull struck a new idea into her head. Inspiration, again. She had not felt so creative in years. "Florida," she said out loud.

Arden took the poems and stuffed them into her back pocket. "Florida?"

"Yes," said Bertha, when she bent to sign the bill. "It just came to me. A slim volume of poems on Florida. You know, the *real* Florida."

"I just got here Bertha. It's *all* real to me."

"That's my point," said Bertha, tucking the receipt into her billfold, "a fresh perspective, the view from outside, from the margins, as it were. And you might even"—she paused, inspiration winging her ever higher—"yes, you might even want to capitalize, just a little, on your very interesting and unique heritage. You could call the book *La Florida*. I can see the cover now." She stood, dismissing the waitress by ceremoniously handing her the ballpoint pen.

"Envision this, Arden." Bertha Michaels waved her hands over the dark waters of the river as if conjuring. "Envision the silhouette of an Apalachicola oyster fisherman standing in his boat, plying his picturesque tongs, while the sun sinks behind him, illuminating—as if they are on fire—letters that say, *La Florida*." She made a little, private humming sound of satisfaction, then, applying just the slightest pressure on Arden's back, directed her up the ramp toward the front door.

Chapter 17
Groves of Academe

The next day Bertha Michaels perched on a white wrought iron patio chair beneath a giant magnolia in her backyard, binoculars trained on what could possibly be a summer tanager. You didn't see them much in town anymore. Not these days. She lowered the binoculars and sat quietly thinking, not for the first time by any means, of yesterday's outing with Arden Benbow.

An uneasy feeling kept rising to the surface, the notion that she may somehow have misconstrued or perhaps even exceeded the orders given her in sacred trust by her superior. But the more she thought about her commission, the less sure she felt about its underlying intent.

She lifted the binoculars again. Kept them trained. Her dominant feeling last night as she had watched Benbow's red taillights disappear into the distance had been: I have accomplished my mission. But what had she done except mentor her, urge her on toward tenure, toward a successful academic life? Probably not what they had intended at all.

And if this was not their intention, what exactly was? If they did not want Benbow to succeed, then did they want her to fail? Certainly they could not fire her. That much was certain, and by the rules.

She lowered the binoculars, watched a hummingbird drink deep from her red buckeye, so deep she could almost feel the crimson liquid in her own parched throat. Observing nature always touched her strangely. Now she felt somehow refreshed, fortified, ready to go on in her assembling of possibility. Ready even to think the dreaded phrase: moral turpitude.

Oh, it had not been used in her own case, but she had sensed it all along, lurking in the dark crannies and recesses of the system like a hidden beast, poised, ready to leap out at her. The possibility of public humiliation.

She had shrunk down to something small, scarcely breathing. Solitary. As she was now.

Quickly she gathered up her things—binoculars, her copy of Peterson, her coffee cup—and hurried through double doors into her living room, sat down in the leather chair, pressed herself against the great breast of her kiva. Breathe, she told herself.

In a moment, she went into the kitchen where she filled a blue glass with water and drank. Deeply. Feeling the water ease past the relaxing muscles of her throat.

She knew now, had known for a long time, that they would never have used moral turpitude against her. Just as they wouldn't use it against Benbow, more than thirty years later. For the simple reason that they would seem illiberal, unsophisticated, small in the eyes of the greater academic world.

She set the glass down on the counter, gazed out her kitchen window into the garden she loved. Meanwhile her mind searched her mental library for a book, a book from the fifties. What was it called? *Groves of Academe*, that was it. Mary McCarthy. In this novel a man of abrasive personality and undistinguished scholarship who was up for tenure had deliberately started the false rumor that he was a member of the Communist party, thus ensuring that they would retain him forever. An indifferent scholar, but an exceptional strategist.

That was the difference between fiction and real life. In fiction the weak might subvert the powerful. In her own life she had not known that to happen. Not ever.

She remembered a professor from graduate school who had said in his seminar on the novel that the protagonist of any fiction must either change himself or change the system. Then, removing his glasses, he had said to them, "The same is true for you." Showmanship, she had thought at the time.

But if it were true, which would Arden Benbow choose? Would she change herself, or would she change the system? Which one was possible for her? And what might *they* do to protect themselves, while still appearing to their own eyes in a graceful light? For they would *do* something.

Through the morning silence ripped the cry of the pileated woodpecker.

Bertha Michaels's naked, expert eye fixed on the dead pine tree she had preserved as habitat. Against the gray bark, red suddenly flashed. Then followed the rat-a-tat-tat of its questing bill. Common name: Godalmighty bird.

Returning resolutely to her station at the kiva, she took up her binoculars for a closer look at whatever might be moving. There was drama here, drama unending. Flight. Struggle. Competition for food. She should check the feeders, make sure she had outwitted the squirrels.

Academe was like that too—an ongoing competition over limited resources. It was the same natural drama, but there was something more, too, an intellectual overlay that fed on complexity and intrigue. Arden had wandered into a world she could not possibly imagine much less comprehend, a world that now had her in its sights, a world whose ways were varied and practiced.

They might simply find her publications insufficient. If she published only poetry they might object that she had no scholarship. If she published only scholarly work they would object that she had not published poetry, the discipline for which she had been hired. Or they might simply arrange things so Arden would *want* to leave. And there were so many ways to do this. They could increase her teaching load, give her assignments out of field, overload her with committee work. The possibilities were endless.

Bertha's Audubon bird clock chirped out the hour, flat and exact. Ten o'clock. What had she done with the morning! She had intended to spend it in her study. She had a paper to write for the American Renaissance Society, a book club lecture to prepare. Important things awaited her attention, obligations. She could not devote her life to Arden Benbow.

She would just check the bird feeders and then get straight to work. But passing the doors into the garden, she paused. Something caught her eye. Something stirring on the Ville de Nance camellia. Yes, it *was* a summer tanager after all. Absolutely. And now that her eyes feasted on the sight she wondered at the bird's rarity. What had become of them all?

And yet she knew. Heedless construction had driven them further and further into the forests, threatening them with extinction. One day perhaps the brilliant, beautiful birds would all be gone, leaving none behind except crows strutting in dark suits, their impatient cries splitting the air.

For now, it seemed, there had been a reprieve. The scarlet tanager was back in the garden, hopping about with bright plumage and distinctive cry, calling attention, oblivious of danger. Bertha Michaels, who had survived for so long only by muting her feathers—requiring little, doing much—wondered what would happen now to the small brown wren couched in the neighboring tree.

Chapter 18
Laundry

The sad-faced man peering through Arden Benbow's rusty screen door said, "I'm your sheetrock man."

"Altron Ringo!" she exclaimed, as if to a long lost relative. Then she remembered Butch warned her not to scare him, that good sheetrock men were as temperamental as they were scarce. Instead of embracing him, she opened the screen door and extended her hand, which he took with some surprise. "Delighted to meet you. Butch said you might drop by."

"Got my gear," he said, nodding in the direction of a chalky blue van with doors tied shut with rope. He was short, lean but muscled and had a faintly equine look, owing to his long jaw and delicate eyelashes. "Butch tells me you're building you a bathroom. Got a tile setter yet?"

She nodded, pulled him through the door and down the hall to the very end, where the sewing room was being transformed. The walls were roughed out, the wiring completed, the plumbing and fixtures in place, including a canary yellow Jacuzzi for Alice. A surprise.

"Going to be a winner," said Altron, in a flat tone. He pulled a tape measure out of his pocket and a thick, gnawed red pencil.

"Well, I was just going to do some laundry," Arden said.

"Don't let me hold you up none," said Altron.

Out on the back porch stood an old wringer washing machine that Butch had said he "might could" get working but never had. He was visiting his ailing aunt in Hayhira today, and Arden needed a change of sheets and some clean clothes. She exposed the machine's innards, lay on her back contemplating, then sat up to reach for a basin wrench when she noticed Miss Hattie sitting in her porch rocker across the field, watching.

What was the protocol here? Should she wave? Should she pretend not to notice her? Last week when she had seen her neighbor carrying groceries down the path toward her cabin, she had been on the point of offering help, of plunging uninvited into her life. But she had held back, uncertain. Later she had regretted it, cursed her reticence. Human interaction seemed so fraught, so labyrinthine here in the South.

She longed again for a guidebook to this foreign country. Then she realized her book on the novel of manners, indispensable for lulling her to sleep each night, was exactly that. For had she not been living in the nineteenth or possibly even the eighteenth century for the past few weeks? Her nightly reading had probably already subtly influenced her behavior. Had she not shown sensitivity and manners in leaving the sheetrock man alone, rather than hanging over his shoulder to watch and perhaps even to offer a few pointers, as she had wished?

Would it violate manners to yell across the field at her neighbor? Come to think of it, she remembered reading that sometimes characters got so exasperated with the perils and insufficiencies of language that they resorted to gestures instead.

Arden therefore stood up, waved at Miss Hattie, who may or may not have nodded in response.

Oh well, ambiguity was going to be a fact of life. She turned her attention back to the washer and in half an hour it was ready for the trial run. She plugged it in, arranged her sheets inside, and turned it on. It groaned into service. Arden glanced across the field. Her neighbor was still there. She seemed to be mending or perhaps stitching squares of a quilt, bright fabric lying across her knees.

The wringer, a technological miracle designed along the lines of a pasta machine, worked perfectly. A little spirited cranking, and clothes snaked out the far side and into her laundry basket. But how to dry them. Three thousand miles away, of course, she had both a dryer and a washer, Fluff and Flo. But today she was having a taste of life on the plantation.

Then she felt it, the seduction of history. She recalled a movie where people boiled clothes outside in giant pots set over blazing fires. Arden was now one with these women, contributing her strength to the common labor, women who had been silenced through the ages and for whom she must now speak. History seemed to take art tenderly into her arms.

The poem Arden envisioned was an interior monologue in which the same woman was washing clothes three different ways at three different times in history. In the final stanza their voices would intertwine, become choral, insistent, demanding justice.

But amidst these musings, unaccountably the voice of Bertha Michaels intruded itself into her brain, telling her yes, write the poem immediately, send it out, only five years remained until tenure review. Suddenly Arden did not want to write the poem at all, and nobody could make her. Besides, she was doing her laundry.

She would hang the clothes in the sun to dry. She remembered as a child helping her mother hang out the wash and later, the sweet, dry smell of sheets and towels as together they folded and stacked them on the dining room table. A Proustean recollection of cotton scorched by a hot iron suffused her. She had not expected to miss her mother, found herself glancing toward the cabin, toward Miss Hattie, as if she needed something.

She needed some rope, actually. Had some somewhere. On her quest she noticed that Altron had set up sawhorses in the dining room and was penciling hieroglyphics onto a section of sheetrock. A tool belt hanging heavily from his slim waist seemed to slow his movement as if he were some kind of diver at a perilous depth. She heard Jimmy Freebeau up in the attic banging and sawing away, finishing up the ductwork for the air conditioning. All this noisy industry made her feel less lonely.

She found the rope in the parlor and a moment later determined the side yard to be the perfect place to hang clothes. But in the absence of trees, what would hold the line up? Then she remembered seeing next to the washing machine several odd forked poles five or six feet high. They must be for holding up the line.

She tied one end of the line to the porch. Then she pulled the hearse around to the side of the house and parked it opposite and tied off the other end of the rope to the door handle. The line, too low and saggy now, would stand up nicely, she knew, with the proper application of those forked poles.

Miss Hattie seemed to be sitting slightly forward in her chair, as if to see better. The sky looked a little cloudy. Crows cawed from the far side of the field. A skill saw screamed, then died into nothing.

That was Jimmy, but maybe she should check on Altron before she tackled the clothes. Inside she found his keyhole saw sticking up out of the sheetrock and his crown-head hammer resting on a bologna sandwich with the crusts cut off and one bite missing. No sign of Altron anywhere. His van was gone.

Out on the back porch she found some clothespins in a rusty red coffee can. Long, graceful, weathered pins, the kind with no spring, the kind she had seen affixed to people's noses in books of nursery rhymes. She liked these clothespins and thought maybe she would write that poem after all, about the three women washing the clothes, and just not tell anybody she had done it.

Emily Dickinson, who was generally right about everything, had once said "publication is the auction of the human mind." Arden vowed to read more Dickinson. In one of those boxes stacked in her studio there must be a volume or two of her poetry. But no, she had been courting distraction again. Her present task was not to write about doing the wash but to actually *do* the wash, a choice which in the long run would probably also make her a better poet.

Quite simply, she would now hang the wash.

She wedged the supports under the line at fixed intervals. True they wavered, but as if by design. What yielded would not break. She hung up the first sheet and stepped back to admire. One of the supports listed a little, then slowly, as if in a graceful faint, it fell forward, lowering the sheet until it rested on patchy grass.

What she heard may have been a laugh or it may have been a godalmighty bird at a distance.

Arden repositioned the support and studied the sky. Definitely more clouds than before but probably nothing important. It usually didn't rain here until two or three in the afternoon, and it was still morning. Late morning. She brushed twigs and dead grass off the sheet and fastened it back on the line.

Jimmy Freebeau came out and asked her where the breaker box was at, and she went inside to find it. The box turned out to be in what she thought was a closet but Jimmy Freebeau knew for a natural fact to be the butler's pantry. Jimmy Freebeau's people on his mother's side were educated and came from money, but you wouldn't hardly know it to look at them today.

Arden loaded up the washer with her socks and underwear. Altron came out at last and asked what happened to the electricity. Where have you been? asked Arden. Lunch, said Altron. At ten thirty? said Arden. When you get up at five, said Altron, elliptically. Arden asked if there was something he could do while the power was off. It's your dime, said Altron.

She hung the second sheet. The sky was beginning to roil a little. She glanced across the field to Miss Hattie's place to make sure she kept faithful watch at her post. Arden muttered a curse at the absent author of the book on the novel of manners and started across the field to test the imperfect communication system.

Miss Hattie waited in her rocking chair on the porch of her weathered house. She sat on a bed pillow, another supported her back. She smelled faintly of baby powder and Niagara starch. In a cardboard box at her feet her sewing was neatly folded. She held a stout cane between her knees in hands, which were the color of polished wood. "Hattie," she said, nodding gravely. "Hattie White."

"Arden Benbow. Your neighbor."

"Yes, you must be," said Hattie, her face suddenly breaking into a smile. "And I don't care what they saying about you, I ain't laughed like this in forty years. June Bug say to me, he say when you movin' in, who be the king of that castle yonder? I say, look to me like just a queen be plenty good enough. I know it to be sufficient here in my own house. Just me living here now."

"I do have a companion. She'll be here as soon as she finds a job. And we've got six kids."

"Ooooh, that many. Land. Don't hear about folks with that size family these days. Used to, everybody had size. Say, where'd that handsome young black fellah go you had around you? I liked him. Is he one of those lady boys? My nephew Ernest is a lady boy down to Pompano Beach. He doing fine. Only one a my nephews ever come to consequence. My sister, his mama, she say, too bad he a lady boy. I say, before the Lord we all just the same. Precious, purely precious in his eyes." She looked up at the sky. "Might be it's fixing to rain." She studied the sheets on the line.

"You don't miss much, do you Miss Hattie?"

"Well, darlin', this right eye, now it might be upsighted. But this left one here, she keep a good watch going. And this chair here"—she slapped her hands on the arms—"my mother's chair, my watchin' chair. You get old, you watch. When you young, you do.

"I done a few things in my life. Yes sir." She paused, studying the clouds as if her history were written there, then laughed gently. "Oh my yes, might be things that make you catch your breath." She shook her head. "Way I see it, now, we all doing the best we know how every living minute. Most of us anyway. Not all. Oh Lord, no, not all." She laughed again but in a different key, this time like a warning rather than an embrace. "I could tell you stories, child. Say, you don't mind, do you, having a old lady keeping watch?"

But words had failed Arden Benbow. Relieved in a way she could not begin to explain, she raised one hand as if it could speak for her, then let it drop by her side.

Hattie looked at her intently for a moment, and then her gaze drove past toward her neighbor's side yard. "Fellah out there waving his arms like crazy over to your place. White man," Hattie said.

"Sheetrock man," Arden managed.

"I wouldn't give you one thin dime for no sheetrock man, black or white, but you better see does he want something. 'Sides," she said, thumping her cane on the porch with amusement, "it be raining on your wash, girl."

Chapter 19
Pleas and Sanka

Like the wise little pig, Provost Regis Factor arrived for breakfast ten minutes early. And like the wise little pig, Factor had a proper appreciation for strategy. Business methods ran this country and there was no reason they couldn't run education too. That's why several years ago President Cager had lured him away from Chicago's B-School to name him provost. He could rest assured that minor problems, like this one now involving the new minority hire, would never catch him off guard or even so much as reach his ears as long as Factor was his point man. Vice President Wintermute, to the president's growing dismay, could not really be counted on for much beyond fund-raising and playing golf with legislators.

Regis Factor was enjoying his solitary coffee in a booth at Midway College's faculty club, having chosen a seat with a view of the entire room, on the side that did not face the glare of subtropical morning sun.

The dean would sit next to him, and opposite him, looking into the light, would sit Booth Hazard, chair of English, and St. John, director of the writing program. St. John preferred to have his back to the wall and liked an unobstructed exit so he could leave quickly. As he would today. The provost had no desire to prevent this departure but only to illustrate its awkwardness, its inappropriateness, by guiding him into an interior seat.

The provost glanced up to see the dean hesitantly standing in the doorway. He motioned him over, and they shook hands warmly and patted each other on the back softly and briefly. In another minute Hazard came in and took his place opposite the provost. The waitress brought coffee.

St. John was late. By virtue of his lateness he would gain a place on the outside. Could therefore slip in and out whenever he damned well pleased. No matter. It was a minor point and the provost's eye was fixed on the greater.

The three men studied their menus, waiting for the fourth. Factor was drawn to the Eye Opener Special—a stack of pancakes, eggs, link sausage. He eased his girth out against his Sansabelt trousers, a way he reminded himself to keep in fighting trim, and ordered instead one poached egg and dry toast. Kilgore, who would never be more than a dean, ordered the Eye Opener. Hazard ordered the eggs benedict and placed his napkin in his lap with prim anticipation.

St. John came in at last, wearing blue jeans, a jacket, a white drip-dry shirt and a red tie festooned with Scottie dogs and fire hydrants. These satiric little concessions to academic convention had always set Factor's teeth on edge: the tie, the jacket, the white shirt. He knew without looking that instead of black wingtips the man wore Birkenstocks, probably with socks. But Factor would seem not to notice, nor would he rise to pat him on the back. Instead he would remain seated and extend his hand in polite greeting.

St. John didn't bother to look at the menu. No, he must interrogate the waitress on each ingredient of his breakfast. The sausage must be Bradley's patty. Nothing else would do. Eggs over, not hard but not runny either. If they contained albumen, he warned her, he would send them straight back. And grits. The man must have grits. Not instant grits, mind. And no cheese in them, above all. Wheat toast with butter, not margarine.

When at last the waitress had been dismissed and Factor had poured St. John some coffee out of the carafe on the table, the provost cleared his throat and began, choosing his words carefully, aware suddenly of the caffeine seeping from the cup by circuitous routes into his bloodstream. Should have ordered Sanka. Hated Sanka. No half measures in anything for him, not if he could help it.

"Well gentlemen," he began, "we are here, as you may have surmised, because of a little problem we have in common."

"It's not my problem," said St. John, taking a crumpled pack of Camels out of his shirt pocket. "I've got better things to do than sit around passing judgment on my colleagues."

Like caffeine, a pure, intellectual loathing rushed through Factor's veins. This was energy he could convert, could use. He directed his eyes as if they were mounted in a turret. "As the director of the writing program, St. John, you would have, I should think, a particular interest in this little problem of ours. Arden Benbow is a player on *your* team."

"*I'm* not even a player on my team. I don't like or believe in teams, as you all well know. I find game imagery infantile at best, dangerous at worst. How you talk determines your reality. Worse yet, it determines mine. This is not Monopoly, boys, nor is it, all evidence to the contrary, even war." He suspended the narrative thread while he lit his cigarette. "You're talking about people's lives here."

"Exactly," said Factor, suppressing a cough.

"Just a minute," said Hazard, straightening his paisley tie, "I must say I feel my motives have been impugned here."

Just then the waitress arrived with four heavy plates, and after a moment's hesitation mistakenly set the dean's Eye Opener Special before Regis Factor who regarded it with some interest. The dean, always slow to assert himself regarding policy and procedure, was nevertheless assertive where eggs and Bradley's country sausage were concerned. He exchanged the provost's poached egg and dry toast for his Eye Opener and set to work with a will.

St. John turned his plate around several times as if steering his Jaguar into a particularly narrow parking place. The eggs must be examined from all angles. Likewise the grits, which earned their own pat of real butter. Next he cut the crusts off his wheat toast, spread all three slices with both butter and grape jelly, rejecting the mixed fruit with animation. As his concluding act, he cross cut his eggs and sausage. The benefit to all this preparation was that he could now consume his breakfast with disgusting rapidity.

The provost caught Hazard's eye, and the latter gave a little shudder of revulsion.

The rest of them had hardly begun eating when St. John pushed his ravaged and nearly empty plate into the center of the table and asked, with an eggy wisp clinging to the corner of his mouth, "So what's it going to be, boys? Fall back and punt? Eh? An end run?" He fished in his pocket for his cigarettes and lit one with deliberation, tossing the spent match toward his plate.

"St. John, will you be serious!" Factor had not meant to raise his voice. The breach stunned him. He felt the table tilting away from him while the power slid toward this man in the outlandish tie, this man who ate but did not work with efficiency, who lit a cigarette before the rest of them could finish. Factor picked up his coffee cup, set it down, shot another glance at Hazard.

Hazard cleared his throat, wiped his mouth slowly and meaningfully with his napkin, then addressed the director of the Writing Program. "One might wonder, St. John, about your own eagerness to defend such a person."

Silence fell. Then St. John said, "Gentlemen, you've been pleased to criticize me in the past, sometimes directly, sometimes through not very subtle innuendo, for my relationships with members of the opposite sex. Am I to understand now that you are criticizing me for an imagined preference for my own sex? You've raised hypocrisy to an almost incomprehensible level, it seems to me." He looked slowly around the table. "Admirable, gentlemen, admirable. I hope now you'll forgive me if I rush off to work on my novel. And please do pardon me too if I admit that the question of whom Miss Benbow sleeps with is not one that greatly troubles or even interests me." He stood, ground his cigarette into a pat of butter, and left.

For a moment there was silence. The partially extinguished cigarette released persistent little smoke signals into the atmosphere. The provost signaled for the waitress to remove the smoldering plate and to bring them a fresh carafe of coffee. For a few minutes they ate without speaking, their cutlery carrying the burden of communication.

Then the provost said, "Well, gentlemen, I think we can get down to business now."

Dean Kilgore's complexion had turned the color of his half-eaten buttermilk biscuit. "I do wish he wouldn't do that."

"The way I look at it is he's been consulted. If his way of dealing with problems is to ignore them, then in my book he's given others carte blanche to take care of things as they see fit. And that's exactly what we're going to do, gentlemen."

Hazard raised both eyebrows, a gesture he used to capture the floor. "What's the game plan?"

Factor refilled their coffee cups, though not his own, and assumed a meditative posture, looking over their heads and across the noisy room, then returning his gaze to them and confessing, "My friends, I've been thinking lately—and I speak as someone trained in business, a relative stranger to the world of art—but I've been thinking, musing, considering the possibility that these fine young people under our guidance really do need more exposure to the arts than we've been providing them. And especially they require exposure to poetry. Poetry writing, I mean, specifically. Say, make poetry workshop a requirement for all undergraduates."

Hazard shook his head. "Haven't got the faculty to handle it, Regis. Oliver's in London all year. That leaves only Benbow, and she's green as grass."

"Also," objected the dean, "it seems to me writing poetry's something you've got to have some aptitude for. You get a bunch of jocks in there and tell them to write a poem, and you're going to have an insurrection on your hands."

"Precisely," said Factor, pushing his plate away. "In fact we could try the plan out on the rugby team this summer, test it. Pilot program, so to speak. Put Benbow in charge of it."

For a moment no one spoke. "There *is* a kind of elegance to it," said Hazard finally.

The dean stared dumbly for a moment, then struggled to speak. "You'd do that?"

"It's not a death sentence, Billy Wayne," said Factor, eyeing the lone sausage link that remained on the dean's plate. "She might learn a little discretion along the way. If she learns that, handles her classes, publishes sufficiently, why then we don't have a quarrel in the world with her. Now do we, gentlemen? That's how diamonds are made, after all, by intense pressure."

The dean pushed his plate away.

Hazard blotted his lips carefully. "Actually I started a little initiative on my own some time ago. My assistant Bertha Michaels has been keeping an eye on Benbow for a couple of weeks now."

"Umm," said Factor, spearing Billy Wayne's abandoned sausage. "Good thinking. Team spirit, Booth. I like that." He looked over at the stunned Billy Wayne Kilgore, whose candidacy for dean Factor had not supported. And time had proven him right. Billy Wayne lacked vision, initiative, the will to lead. Might be better off in the ranks, out of the loop. Give him a small golden parachute, say, and put him back in the classroom where he belonged. The provost sliced into the dean's sausage and chewed thoughtfully.

"And Kilgore," continued Hazard, "I can't think you'd object to Regis's plan. If memory serves, it was *your* wife who sold Miss Benbow that extraordinary house not one mile from campus.

"Warmer?" the chair of English asked, shifting tone and seizing the coffee carafe. Without waiting for a reply, he filled Billy Wayne's cup up to the very brim, where the scorched black liquid remained quivering, barely contained.

Chapter 20
Sheetrock

"We got trouble," said Butch, wedging his head into the cramped attic bathroom that Arden was painting Georgia Peach. She paused, brush uplifted, a smear of paint on the end of her generous nose. "Altron, he knows those two young 'uns of yours get here in a couple of weeks."

"Right. Kip and Jamie. You knew that too."

"Yeah, I knew it, but I'm not like Altron. I can know it and go right ahead like before. But Altron, he says now he's got pressure on him to finish."

Arden waited for Butch to go on.

"You don't know the man like I do. This is how Altron gets just before he quits. I know the signs. Notice how sometimes just his tools are here and not him?"

"Lunch," Arden said. "He goes to lunch sometimes two or three times a day."

"That's not lunch, it's temperament," Butch said. "Artistic temperament. Talk to him, Arden. You're an artist your own self."

"Is he here now?"

"Just barely."

Downstairs Arden found a piece of sheetrock resting across Altron's sawhorses, his keyhole saw sticking up through the sheetrock and his buckled tool belt resting in a perfect circle on the floor as if he had been lifted up bodily out of it by magic hands.

But a quick search revealed him sitting cross-legged on the back porch next to the old washer, gazing out across the field, smoking a cigarette. He had taken off his shirt in the heat, though it was not much past ten in the morning, and for the first time Arden saw beneath his dark ponytail, the lovely, delicate blue spider web tattooed across his back. In the lower right corner of the web sat a stylized, almost geometric red spider, contrasting with the organic sweep of the web.

Arden was instantly enthralled. She sat quietly down next to him. Together they listened, or at least bore witness, to the chatter of squirrels in the neighboring pines and to the slow steady sound of Miss Hattie's hoe tracing its way through her vegetable patch.

"Altron," she said finally, "I have my faults, goddess knows, but I do know beauty when I see it."

"That's just Florida, ma'am." He took his last drag and flicked the butt in a delicate arc out into the side yard.

"I mean your tattoo. I've never seen anything remotely like it. The red spider strikes straight into my heart. And that wonderful blue filigree feathering out toward the edges. Who did it, Altron? Somebody local?"

"No'um. Nobody around here. I got it over to Pensacola. There's this guy named Earl. Just Earl. A lot of those artists don't have but one name. And Earl, he's a real artist, Miss Benbow. That's one man I look up to. I mean, you go in there and he studies you. Intent. You don't tell him what you want done on you. No, that's his prerogative. You are the canvas, and he's the artist. He says to me, he says, 'This here back, Altron Ringo, wants a spider web on it.' And do I tell him no? I do not. It's a question of respect."

"And trust," Arden said.

"You understand me."

"I think I do, Altron. It'd be like this college I work for, say if they were to tell me I had to write poems about Florida, when we've only just met, Florida and I. States are like people, Altron. You get to know them gradually, a day at a time. California I know. We're on a first name basis. But I have no business writing a poem about this perfect stranger called Florida, attractive though I may find her."

"It's for you to say what you're going to do or not do."

"Exactly, Altron."

"And old Earl, he might take one look at your back and get his own idea. Even if you was dead set on a spider web."

"And I would respect that. Each work is unique."

"Miss Benbow, I see you understand a lot about this bidness."

"I'm a poet, Altron."

"Well, let me ask you this, ma'am, artist to artist. Do you ever feel the pressure of somebody waiting on you to just get it done, when what you're aiming at is more than that? See, when I'm on a job, take this one, for instance."

Arden had noticed that in Southern speech, the listener must note these subtle pauses which are almost but not quite questions, and say 'yes' intermittently or at least nod so that the conversation can go forth. She nodded.

"Well," continued Altron, as if suddenly released into communication, "while I'm sheetrocking I'm all the time thinking about the life that's fixing to go on inside these very walls that I put up, and that maybe the way I do it is going to have some kind of—"

"Effect?"

"Yes, effect. You know, like if I get the walls up in just the right way—no lumps or dents, nothing crooked—this family might . . . I mean in a way what you do is going to get mixed up in . . ."

And here she realized he was deeply moved, perhaps to the verge of tears. She struggled silently to remember what she had read about sensibility in her nightly reading. The person of sensibility was finely tuned, emotionally vulnerable, quick to trust and could become isolated through the intensity of her feelings. In a flash Arden saw there was no difference between the heroine of a novel of manners and an artist. She racked her brain for the remedy, which she had read only last night, in prose so turgid and soporific she couldn't recall it now that she needed it. Then the answer came to her. Experience. Suffering was in there too somewhere, in fact a whole chapter's worth. But for Altron that had already happened. Now she needed to engineer some kind of transforming experience for Altron.

What she usually did in an emergency like this was just to start talking, hoping her slumbering wisdom would rouse itself and run after her wagging tongue. "Altron," she said, gazing across the field and noticing that Miss Hattie, as if summoned, had laid aside her hoe and taken her seat on the porch for this little drama. Her straw hat still sat on her head, and she looked curiously formal, as if dressed for the performance. "Altron, you may be taking on too much responsibility."

"Responsibility?" said Altron. "My wife, she says I don't begin to know the meaning of the word."

"It's a complicated word. I think of it as response-*ability*, the ability to respond. You have that. Definitely you have that."

"I do."

"Maybe too much of it." He nodded in melancholy acknowledgment. And suddenly the way opened clear before her, and she knew what to tell Altron. She seemed to be telling it to herself too. "I think we have only one responsibility and that's to shape our art in whatever manner comes to us. We must follow the trajectory of our passion."

He looked at her with tears shining in his eyes that he held back by elevating his chin ever so slightly.

"But I'll tell you what else might help, Altron. Might help us both, actually."

He gave the requisite go-ahead nod.

"Teaching your art to somebody else could do that. Passing it on."

Altron snuffled back the tears in the beginning of relief. The sound resembled a whinny in reverse.

"Think of those Italian fresco painters in the Middle Ages. Nobody knows who they even were! It's like this. If the artist of your spider web—"

"Earl."

"If, say, Earl were run over by a truck tomorrow . . . which, God forbid," she quickly added.

"God forbid," echoed Altron, taking sudden alarm.

"Then you would still be walking around with Earl's art on your back, his design preserved."

"But what if *I* was run over day after tomorrow?" posited Altron.

Arden pondered the question for a moment, but soon regained her momentum. "Then *I* would remember! I will never, ever forget you, Altron, or the art you bear with such reverence on your back. Not ever. And frankly, Altron, they can't kill us all. *Somebody* somewhere will be walking around, remembering Earl's spider web, or if not directly, then my *story* about Earl's spider web, or my daughter's *recollection* of my story. Into infinity."

"That's a real nice way to look at it, Miss Benbow."

"Call me Arden."

"Arden, ma'am."

"Altron, one of the things I like about this vision is I already feel less lonesome. Because let's face it, art can be one lonesome business."

"Oh, I know." Altron shook his equine head from side to side, feeling, perhaps, the halter of responsibility.

"The solution," Arden resumed, trying to gain a headlock on her narrative, for she was speaking considerably beyond what she knew for sure, in the same way she always tried to write beyond it, "the solution is to teach your art."

They both looked startled. "Teach me, Altron, to sheetrock. I mean it. I want to learn."

They stared for a moment into each other's wide eyes. Then Altron said, "Ma'am, I'd be purely honored."

Chapter 21
Hush Puppies

Bertha Michaels leaned so close across the table on the deck at Angelo's By the Sea that Arden smelled her musk perfume. "You know, Arden," she said, tapping Arden's menu with a newly lacquered nail, "you can order that broiled."

Arden sat bolt upright because she was a married woman and because she knew by now, both from her nightly reading and from her limited experiences in the South, that manners constituted an imperfect communication system. Two weeks had passed since her last coastal experience with Bertha Michaels. Did these invitations emanate from Bertha as assistant chair of the department or were they personal? Arden must avoid possible zones of ambiguity.

"Thanks for the advice, Bertha, but I think I'll try the grouper stuffed and fried. I'm interested in the Southern aesthetic that requires everything be cushioned, including food. As if existence has got to be dredged in flour or dipped in batter to blunt any sharp edges."

"I'm glad to see you studying your subject matter, Arden. The outsider always brings a clear eye. Naturally enough you may miss some of the subtleties, you know, what Northrop Frye calls in that wonderful book of his, whose title escapes me right now, though I'm confident I'll remember it later. Probably in the middle of the night." Her gaze wandered off toward the declining sun.

"Northrop Frye, you were saying."

"Oh yes, he calls the manner in which people who share a culture communicate 'the hum and buzz of implication.' They don't speak directly, but they understand one another nevertheless. An outsider will hear but not understand because he, or in this case she, can't intuit the implication. Which is precisely what could make me valuable to you in your work. Though I'm not a native of north Florida myself, after more than thirty years here I am something of a cognoscenti of this strange and rich culture."

Arden looked westward, out past the aptly named Panacea Bridge. The West, where life was simple and direct. She was seized with longing for Alice and all her ways. For a straight-talking, hardheaded woman. Instead, opposite her on the deck of Angelo's sat a woman in a crimson polyester pantsuit and matching lipstick who talked as if she were a secret agent in the employ of several different governments at once.

How had this happened? Why was she here now, in a town called Panacea, instead of in her own living room in Sepulveda listening to the woman of her heart deliver an achingly beautiful cornet solo?

And yet she must somehow stir herself toward sociability, toward humming and buzzing. Like all Austen heroines, she was, after all, a social creature. Resolved, she gulped down some of the sulfurous, chlorinated water provided twenty minutes ago by an ill-mannered high school girl named Ashley, cleared her throat and confessed, not without honesty, "Bertha, I do appreciate your showing me the coast on these little expeditions. It's kind of you."

"Not at all," said Bertha, searching through the ceramic boatload of cellophane packaged crackers for her particular favorite. "Actually this time I do have an ulterior motive."

Confession was delayed by the return of Ashley, from whom they ordered two of the top shelf margaritas. Ashley wrote it down but advised them to go ahead and order dinner now because there was no telling when she could get back to them.

Bertha inquired if the grouper was fresh.

"Oh ma'am, it's *all* fresh," Ashley informed them with more vexation than pride. "Everything on the menu."

Bertha looked dubious, but ordered it broiled, the potato baked.

"And you want the fish stuffed or not?"

"Not," said Bertha, glancing at Arden.

Arden wanted to know what a hush puppy was. Ashley assured her they were real good.

"I know they are," said Arden closing the menu and handing it to Ashley. "I'll have it all. The works. Stuffed, battered, fried, hush puppied and cheese gritted."

After Ashley left, Bertha defined hush puppies and recited their history. She called them "little footballs of fried dough" which began as treats people tossed to their dogs to keep them from begging while their own fish dinners were cooking.

Though drawn toward the metaphoric possibilities, Arden nevertheless remembered that Bertha had been on the verge of saying something that held out at least the remote possibility of directness. Talk of little footballs of dough had worked as a diversionary tactic. The two women sat in silence.

Finally the waitress set down two fluorescent green margaritas. Arden sipped and said, in spite of herself, "Hush puppies in Panacea."

"I thought you'd enjoy that little folk history. In fact, that's one of the things I wanted to talk with you about. Your book I mean."

One of the things. And had they not been over this academic ground on their previous excursion? Certainly there was humming going on but not much implication that Arden could see.

She would buzz back. "My book?"

"Yes, you know, *La Florida?*"

Bertha had raised her voice at the end of her statement so as to transmute it into a question, a linguistic feature she must have learned in her years as a student of Southern culture. Now if Arden nodded, she would not only be agreeing to the continuation of the narrative line, but she would also be accepting the premise of this book, thus moving it a full step closer to obligation, if not reality. But if she said nothing, what would happen then? Would all human commerce cease?

She stared out toward the backlit bridge, listening to the river lapping at the pilings, to the nearly subliminal sounds of a million crustaceans closing and opening in the waning light.

Bertha sipped the green liquid.

Arden sipped.

Bertha cleared her throat. "I refer, of course, to our little discussion, the one we had in Apalachicola, about tenure? We agreed that to make yourself secure in your position you needed to publish a book.

"I could help you," she continued eagerly. "Be your Virgil, as it were, guiding you through the levels of hell. As it were. Or the Paradiso, depending on your perspective." Here she coughed into her napkin.

Arden had been gulping the luminous drink. Her harried mind had sunk into a fantasy in which the author of the soporific book on manners she read each night was sequestered somewhere at a distance, murmuring warnings and appropriate dialogue through a tiny microphone implanted in Arden's ear. She didn't know if she drew the metaphor from sports or from science fiction, but clearly she needed a coach of some kind.

A voice appeared so suddenly at Arden's elbow that for a moment she thought it was the author herself come to save her. Instead it was Ashley with their salads.

"You did want the Greek trim on these," she said, setting down beds of yellow lettuce decorated with purple onion resembling little Olympic Games rings, hot peppers placed strategically at twelve and six o'clock, lumps of feta cheese and the naked limbs of wizened green onions.

"What's Greek trim?" Arden asked.

Ashley sighed deeply, she whom fate had designated to explain the concept of Greek trim to tourists. "It's a dollar and a half extra, and it's already on there."

A feta compli, thought Arden, brightening at her own pun. Dared she say it out loud? Puns tended to breed intimacy. That or hostility.

Instead, she bit into one of the peppers. It bit her back. She chased it with water, then tequila and sat with tears streaming down her face.

"Arden," Bertha said, reaching out her hand. "I don't mean to rush you into anything. I'm just concerned, that's all. About your future, I mean. As it were." Arden nodded but did not take her hand.

The waitress clunked down heavy platters of fish, though they had just received their salads. While Bertha shot annoyed glances at the oblivious Ashley, Arden studied the little footballs of dough. They resembled something from an archeological dig. Their texture seemed distressed, the exterior apparently impermeable. Palimpsests, perhaps. Now the table was covered with thick white plates edged in blue dolphins.

"Shall we have wine?" Bertha asked, before Ashley could escape to the loading dock for a quick cigarette. "Bring us a bottle of the Pouilly-Fuissé, please dear."

Arden took a deep breath and sliced into her stuffed grouper, fighting an impulse to lean close to its fried and battered body and whisper, "I know exactly how you feel."

Bertha chewed with her eyes closed.

Later, when the car purred along 319 toward Tallahassee, Arden stared out the window at moonlight falling across the marshlands, laying down what might be a path to a simpler place. A long-legged, luminous bird searched gracefully, methodically for fish.

Bertha suddenly asked, "Asleep?"

Arden startled. "Just thinking."

"About?"

"Oh, this and that. About my kids and my sheetrock man and Alice's hot tub and the leak around the chimney and my wiring. I can hardly believe it's July already. My two eldest will be here in a week."

"Ah," said Bertha, "then this may prove a godsend after all."

This, thought Arden, sitting up? This? Then they had not yet arrived at the ulterior motive part at all. Until now, the evening had been all hum and buzz. The real thing was coming now, this moment, and here she sat, a complete stuffed grouper resting sideways in her stomach, each dorsal fin embracing an undigested hush puppy.

"A godsend?" Arden managed to articulate. "What may prove a godsend?"

"I hope you'll see it that way. Arden, may I be absolutely honest with you?"

Arden had long observed that people who needed to modify matters of truth with adverbs and adjective were either in trouble themselves or about to inflict great trouble on others. Surely *absolute* honesty was redundant.

"To be perfectly truthful," Bertha continued, "I haven't wanted to discuss this with you . . . have in fact delayed doing so. And I have my own reasons, but—and you must understand this—I speak not as one who creates policy but as the hapless creature who merely implements it."

At last, thought Arden, it comes. Haltingly though. Battered nicely and shaped exactly like a football.

In last night's bedtime chapter, the author, after quoting at length from Jane Austen, had made the point that characters who stammered or corrected or modified their own phrasing were in some way at odds with themselves, with their personal values or perceptions. The cause of the stammering inevitably would be revealed in a couple of hundred pages to the patient and the circumspect reader.

"What I mean to say is," Bertha continued, "I have, they have, rather, the powers that be have seen fit to make a small but significant curricular change that could, or that is to say, that will, have its impact on you. Most probably."

"I don't think I follow."

"It's this, Arden, and I don't quite see how you can turn it down. Once you have tenure, of course, one might hope things could be, would be different. Until that time, and this is certainly true for all of us, until that time, one is obliged, within the context of one's . . ."

"Bertha, to be perfectly honest, you can *just say it.*"

"They want you to teach summer school. Poetic Technique to the rugby team."

"I already have a summer job."

"Really? How can that be?"

"I'm the part-time gardener for Full Court Press. Over near Sumatra. I like it. I'm learning about plants."

"Arden, you must be circumspect about associating with those people. Besides, they can't be paying you much more than minimum wage. You've got to learn to think of yourself as a professional now. I realize after graduate school there's a natural tendency to go on thinking of oneself as a student."

As a human, Arden mentally corrected.

"Besides," Bertha continued, "this summer assignment is a pilot project for a much larger package. Should all go well, the curriculum committee will then develop a proposal requiring every student take a class in poetry writing as a way of acknowledging the importance of the literary arts. Quite a feather in your cap, should that happen. Since Oliver's on sabbatical, that means you'd be in charge, serving as the new departmental fine arts coordinator. Acting, of course, but a start nonetheless."

Arden softly belched her hush puppies.

Chapter 22
Ars Longa

Arden stood on a ladder smoothing with a damp brush long strips of tape between sections of sheetrock. Morning light slanted through the two arches she and Altron had shaped in the east windows, casting figure and shadow onto the opposite wall and from there, bending to illuminate a gently curved space in the hall.

Arden bent her body into the rhythmic work, moving to the country western music Altron required in order to create, though he seemed to have stepped out for lunch.

She liked working with Altron, the ease of it. Even though Altron communicated primarily through grunts, nods and an occasional embarrassed grin, she preferred the company of Altron, and Butch too, over the company of her colleagues. Bertha exhausted her, the dean paralyzed her, the chair distracted her.

Why was that? Half an hour with any of them and she felt sucked by vampires. Or, she thought, shifting metaphors adroitly, it was as if they required energy to drain out of her and into them, replenishing reserves they needed in order to light up their field of play. But what was it, this game they played with such passion? What was its object, and what its rules?

She measured the next section, climbed down and rolled out tape onto the surface of the makeshift table. Altron said three coats of joint compound and these seams would be practically invisible.

And suddenly she remembered a passage she read last night in her book on manners, something about the territory the heroine had to traverse having been rigged up previously with a network of invisible trip wires. She gave a small, mortal shiver.

Up on the ladder again, she resolved to accept the summer appointment—the money would come in handy, might even help the family avoid more debt—but to move slowly forward, testing for trip wires, vigilant for those either who laid them or served those who designed them. She would have to resign from Full Court, though goddess as her witness, she'd much rather work for Boss Granny any day than for Booth Hazard.

Maybe if they didn't give her tenure she'd become a landscape gardener or even a sheetrocker. Either job seemed like honest, good work for a poet. And as she feathered the compound over the tape with her joint finishing knife, she thought about sheetrock, about the way it shaped and defined space for the inhabitants, how it could be both ephemeral and lasting, like poetry itself. Next thing she knew she was writing a poem about sheetrock and poetry right up there on the sheetrock itself, using Altron's thick, red pencil and it was coming like crazy, straight out, the way she liked it.

She sensed Altron come into the room. He simply stood below, not saying anything, waiting, one artist respecting another. And she could keep going because she had learned to write through even children, when the muse was breathing, as now, upon her neck.

Finally she finished, handed Altron his pencil.

"We can cut around her, you know," Altron said, slipping the pencil into the bib of his overalls. "Lift her right out. Patch and tape that hole up and nobody'll be the wiser."

"You know, Altron, I think I'd rather leave it right where it is, covered up, but *in* there."

"Like them medieval fellas you was talking about and their painting and all? Just nobody knowing who did what."

"Yes, exactly. You and I will know it's there. And somebody, maybe in a hundred years, will find it and wonder who made it, but it really won't matter."

Quietly she climbed down. Arden and Altron stood together not speaking, contemplating time and art when Butch came in.

He cleared his throat, out of politeness. "Y'all 'bout done in here?"

"Butch," said Arden, "can we cover this poem over with paint?"

"Well now, why don't we just erase it, then paint? Get good coverage, that way."

"I want it there, inside, permanently."

"Oh, I get you. Like one of them space age time capsules folks will dig up in a thousand years. We might could do her using some of that new kind of paint with the light plaster base. It don't exactly go with your style of house, you ask me. Then again . . ." He paused, noting the new arches at the doors and windows and over the canary yellow Jacuzzi. "It *is* kind of a Mexican bathroom, come to think of it. Why not? Sure, we can do her."

"Olé," said Altron, in his flat yet somehow ecstatic voice.

Chapter 23
Fringe Benefits

The path to the Fringe Benefits Office had proved obscure and circuitous. Arden asked directions a dozen times, but now, at last, she stood before Minnie Lee Philpot, who motioned her around the counter and offered a chair next to her desk.

"You're the new poetry prof, I guess. Coke?" she offered, cranking a thick wad of papers and carbons into her IBM and typing furiously. "I got the papers on your mortgage the other day. Now you're theirs, signed, sealed and delivered." She looked up momentarily, her mouth a little askew, her henna colored hair disheveled.

"Now I'm whose?" she asked, declining the Coke, accepting the chair.

"Oh, you know. The boys." She yanked the papers out of the typewriter. "Now raise your right hand and sign this. It swears in quadruplicate you'll defend the state of Florida against all enemies."

Arden looked doubtful.

"Look honey, you aren't going to get your paycheck without that signature. And that's the simple truth."

Arden raised her right hand, promised to defend Florida, signed the paper and pushed the pen back to Minnie Lee. "Maybe I'll have that Coke after all."

"It's a fine Southern narcotic," said Minnie Lee, standing and smoothing the wrinkles out of her yellow dress. "We're all high on it half the time." She dropped some coins in an ancient machine leaning against the wall of her small office.

Arden took the pale green bottle from her and held it against her face, then took a swallow.

"Yeah, it's hot as hell in here," said Minnie Lee, settling back into her typist chair. "Here on the fringe, that is. The boys can't be troubled with keeping this place cool long as they got their fancy offices up high and their fancy furniture and their fancy secretaries. Here sign this one too."

Arden signed. Minnie Lee fed another form into the machine.

"Now how many dependents you got? This is your health insurance we're working on now."

"Seven, counting Alice."

"Alice is adopted?"

"Six kids, and Alice is my . . ."

"Your?"

"Lover."

"Whee dog!" exclaimed Minnie Lee, riding her wheeled chair away from her desk and into the wall. "I have lived long enough!"

"Apparently," said Arden.

"Oh, no offense," said Minnie Lee, gliding her chair back to its place. "Honey, I lived six years in Tampa. Nothing could surprise me. But the boys . . . oh, those boys." She was laughing now, and struggling against tears. "Someone's ox is in a ditch for sure and certain."

"It might be my ox in that ditch, Minnie Lee."

Minnie Lee turned sober. "Well, that's true enough, honey. I'm really sorry. If it was up to me—"

"If Alice were my husband—"

"Well of course. That would be another story. But as things stand, Alice is not related to you."

"Of course she's related to me. We have made the deepest kind of commitment to each other. I called her my lover for lack of a better word. She is, in truth, my heart's eternal companion."

"To the State of Florida, eternal companion is not the same thing as spouse. They're going to say she's not related to you, and they'll keep on saying it till the cows come home. You can count on it."

"I can't think Florida would treat me that way after I swore to defend her against all enemies. It was not a hard promise to make, Minnie Lee, and I do not take it lightly. You have to understand I fell in love with Florida at first sight."

"Well, honey, this is the clearest case of unrequited love I've seen in a long, long time. You're not ever going to get the state or the college to agree that Alice is your spouse. Not for health insurance, not for retirement. Life insurance we can do. Anybody can be your beneficiary. A dog even."

Arden stood wearily and drained the rest of her Coke.

"We're not through yet, sugar," said Minnie Lee. "Let's get done what we can do."

"And kiss the rest goodbye?" Arden sank back into her chair and picked up Minnie Lee's pen.

Afterward, she was glad she had not brought the car, although a hearse might have seemed appropriate enough after the scene in Fringe Benefits. Striding home the three miles, first on asphalt, then on dirt, past the rugby boys, then a field of grazing cows to the crossroads might do her good.

To the natives, she must look crazy, a lone woman walking in the heat of day, no hat, striding along in a fury, her ox in a ditch, this very ditch. She kicked a rock into it.

A car passed slowly, its passengers marking her and her strange ways. She would never belong here. Bobbi June had said as much, that families in Midway for two or three generations were still considered outsiders, other. Sitting across from Minnie Lee Philpot, trying to account for her life in a way that a printed form could accommodate, she had known herself to be not only alien but illegitimate. Outside the law. Not an hour ago she had sworn to protect Florida, knowing in her heart of hearts that *she* was the enemy.

Another car slowed, sped up. A hawk cried, circling overhead, spiraling on updrafts. For a long time Arden stood in the dusty road, watching spread wings trace invisible forms onto the sky, then disappear at last into bleached and distant light.

Chapter 24
Long Distance

That same evening, three thousand miles away, Alice smoothed the last of Jamie's T-shirts into a suitcase and snapped it shut. Tomorrow afternoon, daughter and son would both be in their mother's presence, emissaries of Alice's love. And it was a good thing, too, since something was clearly going on, something Arden was not discussing in their phone calls. Strange how telephones seemed to compound distance rather than obliterate it.

Alice wandered into the kitchen and filled the teakettle with water, then dumped out half of it. Hard to remember Arden was gone, even when she was so much on her mind. The flame huffed up. She set out a cup, a spoon, one tea bag, then gazed out the kitchen window into blackness.

Maybe she should just call a halt to the long distance job search, quit her job here in L.A., pack up the rest of the household goods and gods and head east with the children.

A leap in the dark.

The kettle whistled. Alice poured in steaming water, contemplated the process of steeping. Was she not ready? Something held her here. But what?

Practicality? Part of it. Lord knows they needed two salaries to live on. Arden thought her salary was handsome, and in a way it was. More than she had ever made, certainly. But it wouldn't be enough for all eight of them to live on with any degree of comfort. At least not for long.

What else? She bobbed the tea bag up and down absently. Fear. Yes, she would have to own it. Fear.

Fear of having no live opera, fear of Southerners, fear of poverty, fear of cows, fear of iceberg lettuce, fear of isolation. Fear, perhaps, of living so far from Chowder, who was, when all was said and done, her dear friend, her confidant. Though God knows the two of them were different enough, never a go as husband and wife. Friends.

She held the tea bag dripping over the kitchen trash. Fear of Arden?

Her mind wanted to dodge the question, shoot down a side street. "No," she said aloud to it, startling herself in the quiet house. "Stop."

"Don't shoot!" called out a familiar voice.

"Topaz," said Alice, carrying her tea into the living room. "I thought you were with Tom."

"I thought I was with Tom too," he said, sinking down onto the couch. "Both of us were wrong. All three of us, maybe."

Alice put the cup of tea into his hands and sat down next to him.

"I was just thinking about Chowder."

"Yeah, him too. There's another sunk relationship."

"Well, it turns out we make perfectly good friends. It's just the other thing we couldn't manage."

"You can afford to be generous and philosophical. You've got Arden."

"She and I don't seem to be communicating very well just now."

"She doesn't want to worry you, is all. She's beleaguered. The house, the job, the South with its strange people and their even stranger ways. You'll be fine once you get there. Both of you will be fine. The kids too."

"But she should tell me. I can't help thinking something's wrong."

"It's just that she feels responsible."

"Responsible?"

"Yeah, like if you've got to give up your wonderful job and move to the end of the earth for her, then she needs to make the end of the earth nice for you before you get to it. And I don't just mean the Jacuzzi bathtub, either."

"Jacuzzi?"

"Oh damn," he said, clapping his hand over his mouth, "that was supposed to be a surprise. Well, you get the idea. It smacks a little of pride, but it's basically sweet."

"I know," Alice agreed. "Profoundly and fundamentally sweet."

"You're a lucky woman," said Topaz, sipping Alice's tea. "I should be half so lucky."

"Well," said Alice sinking comfortably into the couch, "no one could deserve it more. But in the meantime, your room here is just as you left it. And as you can see, I could use the company."

"Coming from a mother of six, that's a big compliment, a very big compliment." He gave Alice's left temple a kiss then leapt up and strode toward the kitchen. "Now what've you got in your freezer for the broken-hearted?"

Chapter 25

Going to the Dogs

"Alice wants us to call her as soon as we get to the house," said Jamie, squeezing her mother's hand, while the three of them stood watching the airport baggage carousel rotate in an apparently endless circle.

Arden's glance fell on a familiar face. On the opposite side of the carousel stood Professor St. John, director of her miserable program, next to a woman with makeup clearly visible at a hundred paces and wearing enormous red hoops in her ears, a woman whom St. John might at any moment marry and endow with his health insurance, even his pension plan, no questions asked. On a whim.

Arden engaged Kip in rapid-fire communication about the dog and rabbits, but too late, here he came now, the locus of privilege.

Arden took a quick breath, made a firm resolve, and politely said, "Professor St. John, these are my children, Jamie and Copernicus."

"Good Christ, you've got kids!"

They stood staring for a moment. Then Arden said, "Actually, six. This is only the advance guard."

She directed Kip to see about the pets and Jamie to watch for the bags, while St. John recovered from the shocking knowledge that lesbians reproduce.

"I just wanted you to know, Benbow," he said at last, "that I didn't have anything whatsoever to do with it. My hands are clean."

At first Arden misunderstood what "it" was. She assumed he was talking about her health insurance. Then she suspected he was talking about much more.

As if in acknowledgement of the potential complexity, he stipulated, "I mean about your summer assignment. The poetry-for-ruggers thing. Not my idea at all. For Christ sakes, you know that I don't even believe writing *can* be taught let alone that it *should* be taught."

"Yes," she said, "I do seem to remember something to that effect."

"Well," he said, acknowledging the lovely lady across the revolving suitcases who was now gesturing for his assistance, "got an out-of-town guest to take care of. Guess I'll see you at the dean's little shindig next week. Rite of passage kind of thing, you might say. Professional obligation and all that. Well, best of luck then."

"Best of luck to you too, sir," she said, moving over to help Jamie with their luggage.

On Thursday she and the children arrived at the Kilgores' house the precise moment St. John opened the door of his flame-colored Jaguar for his out-of-town guest.

"We meet again," said St. John, nodding his head at Arden and her entourage, then noticing with a little start the family's curious vehicle.

"My mother maintains that people keep running into each other when there's something they haven't been saying but are supposed to," remarked Arden, in conversational Southern.

"To be sure," said St. John. "And this is Verna Pepper. Verna, Arden Benbow, our new poetry hire."

"Charmed," said Arden, accepting Verna's outstretched hand and instantly feeling blood red vampire nails digging into the back of her hand. Then just in time Bobbi June, beaming, opened the door on them all.

"Well, come on in, you darling things, you," said Bobbi June. "Arden, honey, introduce me to your precious children."

St. John and Verna squeezed by while Arden introduced Jamie, fourteen, and Kip, thirteen. After the precious children escaped outside to look at the swimming pool, Bobbi June said, "Why Arden, they're beautiful, absolutely beautiful. You never did brag on how adorable they are, with all that gorgeous red hair. They must look just exactly like their father."

"No," said Arden, "they don't. They look just exactly like Alice. Except for their hair."

Bobbi June shot her what might have been a warning glance. "Well, now, sugar, you need a drink."

She led Arden into the kitchen, where she had been squirting bright yellow paste into hardboiled egg halves and decorating their tops with a shake of paprika. "Now what's the matter, honey? You look like you been sitting in a bed of fire ants."

"Where's my drink?"

Bobbi June blushed. "I can do a lot of things, but actually I never did learn how to mix drinks. Billy Wayne's just always done it, and he's out there cooking on the barbecue right now."

"Billy Wayne has cost Alice my health insurance and my retirement benefits."

"Surely not!"

"Well, not Billy Wayne exactly."

"'Course not. He would never do such a thing."

"He would never *know* he did such a thing." Arden searched through kitchen cabinets until she found a glass. "Now look, pour in about two fingers of gin."

"Arden, honey, what are you doing?"

"Teaching you how to mix a drink."

"Well, do the two fingers go up and down, or do they go sideways? And what do you mean about Alice's health insurance and benefits?"

"On second thought, let's use a jigger. Where's the jigger?"

"What's a jigger, sugar? You mean one of those teeny tiny glasses?"

Bobbi June began flinging open doors in the upper cabinets. "All families get health insurance. That's the rule. You have responsibilities, same as Billy Wayne. Is this a jigger?"

"Minnie Lee Philpot says—"

"Shoot, that Minnie Lee. She's forever trying to stir up a nest of hornets. Now what do I do? Fill this up with the gin?"

"Yes, to that second line, then pour it into the big glass, put in a few cubes, top the whole thing off with quinine water and a wedge of lime, if you've got one, a lemon if you don't. Do you realize I had to swear to defend Florida against all enemies just to get my paycheck? What's that about?"

"It's not like Billy Wayne makes the rules," said Bobbi June, stirring the drink and handing it to Arden.

"No, he just enforces them."

"Who just enforces what?" asked Billy Wayne, who had wandered into the kitchen dressed in a chef's hat and matching apron inviting the world to "Kiss the Cook." Arden gave an involuntary shudder, which out of respect for Bobbi June, she suppressed. Black dress slacks and black wingtips completed his ensemble.

"What's this about Arden's health insurance and Alice not being on it," Bobbi June asked.

"We're not here to talk shop. This is a damn party."

"I don't think you said hello to Arden, Billy Wayne."

"I nodded at her from the grill. I can't be everywhere at once." His eyes fastened on the gin and tonic now passing from the hand of his wife into the hand of the unfortunate new hire. "There's beer and wine for the guests. There's no call for you to be mixing drinks. You're out of your depth with that, Bobbi June."

"I expect," said Bobbi June, "that if you find yourself capable of cooking patties and dogs in that ridiculous hat, then I might find myself capable of learning how to mix a little old drink, Billy Wayne. After all, we provide our guests with what they want. Now don't we? Otherwise we could not claim to know what hospitality is."

She turned to Arden and gave her a meaningful look. "We'll be out in just a minute, sugar pie. You go on ahead, and for lord's sake enjoy yourself."

Arden grabbed her drink and escaped to poolside.

Kip and Jamie were being interrogated by Bertha Michaels, in white slacks and lavender silk blouse, and an elderly lady in thick glasses wearing a gauzy flowered dress. The elderly lady kept saying, "My now. My now." The tremor in her head told Arden she must be Helen Core, the retired Shakespeare scholar.

Arden greeted Bertha and introduced herself to Helen Core, who said, "My now."

"I was just asking these charmers of yours," explained Bertha, "where they'll be going to school in the fall. They tell me they'll be going to public school."

"My now," said Helen Core.

"I'd have thought you would have signed them on with North Florida Christian. A little conservative politically perhaps, but it's a school with an exceptional reputation. The public schools here are abominable, Arden, from what I hear."

Helen Core raised an index finger, her head trembling, and said, "My now."

"We've talked it over," said Arden. "They'd prefer public school."

Bertha turned to Kip and Jamie and said, "Mama and Daddy might be in a position to know better than you, mightn't they?"

"Mama and Alice," corrected Jamie. "And I'm not a Christian."

"She's a Taoist and I'm a Buddhist," explained Kip. "Can we go swimming now?"

"Oh my," said Helen Core.

"Ask Bobbi June," said Arden.

"In the big hair and blue eyelids?"

"Bobbi June is your hostess and my friend."

When they ran off to find Bobbi June, Arden sank down in a lawn chair and said, "I hate academic parties."

"Oh my," said Bertha.

"I do too," agreed Helen Core with sudden lucidity. "And I've been waiting thirty-seven years to hear somebody say so."

Just then Booth Hazard came over, obviously ill at ease without a tie. His right hand kept wandering up to his white throat where his starched Hawaiian shirt stood open. "Greetings, Arden. Have you met our Miss Core?"

"Oh my," said Miss Core. "I've got to go home right away. Yes, I know Arden very well. Please excuse me, all of you." She tottered around the pool deck toward the house.

"A shame," said Hazard. "What a noble mind is here o'erthrown."

"Not quite," said Arden, sipping her gin and tonic. "Besieged, maybe. O'erthrown, never."

"Beg pardon?" said her chair, his eye wandering from her effervescent mixed drink to his own warming beer.

"She said, 'quite right'," Bertha quickly interpreted. "I must confess it's always a moving sight to see what happens to a woman who devotes her life to her profession."

"Which reminds me, are we all set to go with the poetry classes this Monday, Miss Michaels? Bertha, that is." Then turning to Arden, the chair said to Arden, "You'll find our students quite remarkable."

"That's putting it mildly," said St. John, sticking his head but not his body into the little circle. Then he guffawed and drifted off to join another group.

"You're aware, I'm sure, that most of our students come from affluent homes but have histories of difficulties with previous institutions. They represent a particular demographic and a particular challenge. Historically speaking, any successes we have in the trenches tend to be well appreciated and even rewarded by the parents, through trusts, behests, endowed chairs, fellowships and the like."

And Mercedes-Benzes, thought Arden.

Kip and Jamie cannonballed into the pool. Guests jumped aside.

"Yes," agreed Bertha, "teaching has always been important at Midway College."

"And let us not forget research, Miss Michaels."

"I meant to say teaching and research, of course, sir."

Arden, who had been keeping an eye on her children in the pool, was contemplating joining them, fully clothed, when Bobbi June tottered onto the patio in her heels, looking a little flushed about the face.

"It's just come to me who's missing from my party. It's Topaz Wilson. I know you miss him, Arden honey. We can none of us have too many friends. Isn't that right, Booth? But you never did get a chance to really know Mr. Wilson."

"No, fate deprived me of that pleasure. Just a nod in passing."

"Well he does have the most remarkable sense of humor," she recollected.

"And irony," Arden added in the tone of lime.

"That too," said Bobbi June, whereupon they were interrupted by the sound of Dean Billy Wayne beating the triangle summoning them to dinner. He had removed the hat in question, but Arden observed for the first time that the apron tied around her dean's ample girth bore the icon of a delighted cow who, unlike herself, was apparently unconcerned for its own fate in a rapacious world.

Bobbi June guided Arden straight for the platter of charred patties and shriveled wieners.

"But I'm a vegetarian," objected Arden, reaching for a stuffed egg. "Don't you worry about me, Bobbi June. I'll be fine."

"Honey," said her friend, "I *know* you'll be fine. You've got to be patient with Billy Wayne, though. Just think of him as a work in progress, like I do."

Chapter 26

Sartor Resartus

"Here now, Arden honey, just turn yourself around so I can get a good look at you in that pantsuit." Bobbi June backed off for the long view of Arden Benbow in the three-way mirror at Southern Inspirations. "Now Bertha, tell the truth. Are those cuffs just a tad too long?"

"Not a bit. She looks distinguished, I say."

"There's an infinity of me going off in three directions at once, and I don't recognize any of us. I do know that we all hate powder blue."

"Well, I don't hate it. You'll find it has a calming effect on the students."

"I don't want to calm them, Bertha. I want to ignite them."

"Turn," commanded Bobbi June. "Bertha, what do you think?"

"It's perfect. She needs the pale yellow one as well. They'll both look wonderful with that skin of hers."

"They'll look like uniforms."

"They *are* uniforms, Arden. They'll identify you as a professional. Bobbi June always looks professional when she goes to work."

"That's right, Arden honey. Why, I wouldn't think of leaving the house without my Big Bend blazer and my face on. 'Course you'll probably leave out the face part."

"A little makeup would be a splendid touch. Especially considering the hair."

Arden ran her hand through her growing hair. "Look, are we done here? My motorcycle's due for delivery any minute."

"Now Miss Hattie told you she'd take care of it, sugar. Let's go get us a nice lunch somewhere, just us girls. What do you say?"

"She'll take both of the suits," said Bertha to the saleslady. "The yellow and the powder blue."

That night Arden, dressed in jeans and T-shirt, lay under her newly shipped motorcycle, changing the oil. Jamie and Kip were in their beds reading, the frogs were in voice and Arden had found inside one of the Harley's saddlebags, wrapped in purple tissue paper, a tortilla press and a love letter from her Alice.

Recollecting the words now, she sighed, smelled—what was it? Smoke! She jumped up, spun around sniffing the air, saw flames at Miss Hattie's kitchen window. Her feet pounded toward her neighbor's place. At the side of the house she found the old woman pulling on a snarl of hose. Arden shook the knots free, turned the faucet on full force, and exploded into the kitchen spraying water over the range and kitchen curtains.

"My land, my land, my land . . ." Miss Hattie stood behind her in the doorway, shaking her head. "Praise Jesus you was by. Praise Jesus, I got me a neighbor. What would I do without you come to help out?"

"Miss Hattie, now you go sit on your porch while I clean up this mess."

"Leave it. Leave it, child. Cleaning is what I know best. You leave it to old Hattie to fix this all up right as rain. Mind you don't tell anybody though. There's folks might want to clap me up inside one of those mental houses. Send me to Chattahoochee for sure. I ain't mental. Anybody might have them a grease fire. You know that."

"I do know that, Miss Hattie. But let's go outside now where we can breathe." She took her by the elbow and guided her out onto the front porch.

"Yes, we'll set out here while the smoke goes on by. Praise Jesus. Now you get comfortable here on June Bug's stool. I'm afraid I got to have my watchin' chair. Old bones. They stiffen up on me these days. How old do you reckon I am?" she asked, settling into her rocker. "I don't guess you'd ever say eighty-seven, now would you? But I make out. I do."

"I appreciate your help with the motorcycle today."

"Big old thing. Smells too. What you want with that anyhow?"

"It keeps me sane, Miss Hattie."

"We got to have that, I know. My garden now, it's the same thing, I expect. Staying right with yourself inside of your own head." She thumped her cane three times on the heart of pine floor. "This here's the truth as I know it. We are truly blessed. Amen."

"Amen," said Arden softly.

Chapter 27
Pedagogy

On Monday Arden stood in front of her first class as assistant professor of English and creative writing at Midway College wearing her uniform, the powder blue polyester pantsuit.

The suit's fibers were not breathing and neither was Arden. Her class was located in a well-appointed but stuffy temporary building not a hundred paces from the construction site of the new Fine Arts Building, where Bertha predicted in four or five years and with any luck at all her young colleague would be installed as departmental fine arts coordinator. In the meantime Arden was "acting," in that capacity and, it seemed, in every other capacity there was or that anyone at all had been able to think up for her.

The students sat in rows, conversing happily with one another, apparently oblivious of her existence. All were male, all white, and all possessed of necks as big around as her waist. They wore T-shirts, shorts and flip-flops. The latter she had only this morning discovered to be onomatopoetic.

She cleared her throat and glanced significantly at her watch. No response. So, placing her first and third fingers into her mouth she emitted an ear-splitting whistle.

She had their attention.

Today and every day she would appreciate their arranging chairs in a circle. They groaned, dragged their chairs around slowly and with sound effects.

She had planned to begin with a question, though she was by nature skeptical herself of answers. A good question, she believed, had the power to engage anyone, for people were by nature curious. "What," she asked, "is poetry?"

"A new requirement," called out yellow flip-flops. Laughter.

"What else?"

Nothing else, apparently. She decided to try a little free writing on the topic. On the board she hastily chalked out three thought-provoking activities: 1) complete the sentence, "Poetry is . . ." 2) answer the question, "What does it mean to live the life of a poet?" and 3) describe your own greatest gift.

She had planned that this would take them an hour when in fact it took them seven minutes flat. She glanced through their sheets of ripped out spiral notebook paper, searching for stimulating responses to share with the whole class, replies that would generate discussion.

Under "Poetry is . . ." she read, among other things:

useless

sissy bullshit

a rip

In response to the question "What does it mean to live the life of a poet?" she read:

swell babes?

death by boredom

food stamps

Under three, their own greatest gift, she read the names, models, special features and colors of a dozen different sports cars.

"There seems to be a fair amount of contempt floating around here today. Contempt is easy enough. Respect is harder. Let's go for what's hard." They all looked at her. "I'd like to know what we're doing here."

An unshaven youth laughed. "You're the teacher. We're just here because the dean says we have to take this summer class to stay eligible."

"Well, we're all part of a little experiment then, I suppose. Not a great reason."

"It's not like we're guinea pigs," said yellow flip-flops.

"Suppose we are," said Arden. "The question might then be how do we make good use of this time? How can we make ourselves and our lives significant? That's what poetry's about anyway. Making sense out of the world. Creating significance."

"It's about a bunch of pointy headed intellectuals sitting around and staring at their own navels, if you ask me."

"You are?"

"I'm Mike. Michael. Michael Rosen."

"Well Mike, what if I were to tell you poets are active people who have an active and very real place in the human community? That they're outdoor people who make real things. Useful things."

"What's useful about poetry?"

"And you are?"

"Bryan."

"Bryan, would you say a telescope is useful? A window? A microscope?"

"You can't eat a poem," observed a particularly heavy young man wearing a numbered jersey.

"Yes, you can," returned Arden. "Poems feed you. In fact one of my favorite poems recreates the experience of eating a Godiva chocolate. It's better than chocolate. It's not fattening."

The circle of men laughed. Arden slipped out of her polyester jacket. "So what I'm proposing is this. Let's give each other a chance. You're athletes, and I accept that. I'm a poet, and I'm asking you to accept that. Let's find an area of overlap, where poetry and athletics converge."

"More like they're opposites," said Bryan.

"History says you're wrong. In ancient Greece there was a well-revered athlete who was also a celebrated poet. In fact his poetry was mostly about sports."

"Name of what?" asked Eugene.

"Name of Pindar," she replied.

More laughter. Arden eased off her tight shoes. "Let's make this brief time together valuable. If we do that, then we win. We're not anybody's lab animals if we're making our own decisions about what counts. I tell you poetry counts."

"Rugby counts," said Michael Rosen. "It's why I came to Midway in the first place."

"You came because you flunked out everywhere else, same as the rest of us," Bryan corrected. "And because your parents said no more football for you."

"Okay," said Arden. "Let's agree that poetry and rugby are it. They're what we care about. They're what we do and who we are. Like Pindar, we embrace poetry and athletics. We celebrate them, and in celebrating them, we celebrate ourselves."

That afternoon found Arden pressed against the womb-like exterior of Bertha Michaels's cool kiva chimney waiting for a cup of mint tea. She was still breathing hard, as if she had run a marathon.

"I know how you feel," called Bertha from the kitchen. "It's the same with the Renaissance." She came in carrying the tea tray and set it down on a small table between them. "To those young men it's as if learning is an imposition."

"We got off to a terrible start," admitted Arden, picking up the blue ceramic cup. "Then I think I did make contact with them. A little. It may just have been the polyester suit, but I thought for a while my heart was going to fly apart under the stress."

"Don't let it," warned Bertha. "Just do your best one day at a time. Cultivate your own interests. Eat well, take vitamins, survive until retirement. That's my goal." She gave a little laugh and picked up the matching sugar bowl.

"Is it enough to live on?"

"Retirement?"

"No," said Arden, waving her hand before her eyes. "I mean, is it enough to live on *now*. Trying to overcome that resistance every single day of your life, defending what you naturally love, what you always have loved."

"Except weekends and holidays," added Bertha, "which are your own. Or rather, they are for your own researches. And that can be a joy, too, Arden, believe me, if you plan them well. Crashaw and I have had some very good times together, I can assure you." She swirled sugar into a blue vortex in her cup. "And there's your lovely, lovely book to think of, to sustain you."

Chapter 28
Greek Trim

That night she couldn't sleep. For the first time in her life Arden Benbow dreaded the morrow. She would have to face the ruggers and somehow lead them to embrace Pindar and his manly poetry. But she had never been very good at fixing up friends with blind dates. Besides, Pindar alone could never do the job. She needed an additional strategy, she was sure, one that was now playing around somewhere in the outer reaches of her mind where she could not lay hands on it.

She jumped out of bed and began pacing the floor in her pajamas. She stubbed her toe on an object barely discernable in the faint moonlight—the damn book! What good was criticism when it came to real life problems! The author was just another expert in a world of experts, offering endless advice and analysis. She decided to fling this book clean into the next county. But just as she opened wide the window, she heard a cow moo. She stopped, her arm drawn back.

That was it! Cows and boys. After class today she had gone to the library to check out editions of Pindar. Coming out into the waning afternoon light, several volumes pressed to her breast, she had seen the rugby boys tracing obscure patterns on the vibrant green field as they ran to and fro, chasing after one another and a strange, wobbly ball that looked for all the world like a giant baked potato. Beyond them, old Mr. Crum's cows stood at pasture, their massive shapes curiously outlined. Something about the boys and the cows and the grass and the angle of light pulling them all together into one vision had stopped her dead in her tracks. She had said out loud, beautiful. Just that, without quite knowing what she meant.

And the moo tonight had carried her backward in time to that moment, where she could put things together.

Boys and cows, she chanted now, standing at the bedroom window in her pajamas and holding aloft the forgotten book. Boys and cows were the same. They wanted sunshine and good food. These boys needed air, and green grass (or in their case, food) and labor designed to satisfy their needs. And what could be simpler to provide? Did they not all live, after all, in the fecund heart of Florida? And was she not now undisputed mistress of Crossroads Gardens?

She grasped the book in her hand and spun around and around like the Olympic shot-putters she has seen on television, then hurled the book far out into the night, in an act of purest joy. Boys and cows, cows and boys. Beauty, she murmured. Just this.

And she shut the window down tight, ready for tomorrow's class. Perhaps now she could sleep.

Across the field an old woman had been planting by the young, waxing moon, her movements slow, supported by a stout cane. Bending down, she nestled seeds into the shape her hand made in the soil, tamping with her cane, straightening, moving on. At the sound of the window opening, she stopped and listened. Then against the roar of her neighbor's new air conditioner, Hattie White heard the thud of something striking the ground, then a window closing.

She bent back to her labor, the planting called for by this new moon.

Chapter 29
Crossroads Gardens

Arden flattened down on her Harley, speeding with a light heart toward poetry and her ruggers. Today she would introduce them to Pindar and who knew what else. Blessed, she murmured into the wind. The world pays me to read Pindar and talk about poetry.

The young men had dragged their chairs into a circle and were talking rugby when she came in. Their teacher had forsaken her powder blue polyester suit and instead wore faded but immaculate jeans and a rugby shirt. She carried a motorcycle helmet of midnight blue in one hand and a saddlebag filled with editions of Pindar in the other. Her step was elastic. She pulled up a chair and passed around the books. They all issued forth the obligatory groan.

Then they began to read. First they read to themselves and then they talked about running, about track, about passing the baton. About how passing the baton was a thing called a metaphor and how there were metaphors in poetry. Had to be. Then Michael read a poem out loud, Eugene read another, Bryan another.

On Monday, when they met again, it would be at their teacher's house, a place called Crossroad Gardens, just west of the rugby field. Planting lettuce, it turned out, was no different than writing a poem.

Chapter 30
Small Change

Arden stood at her new kitchen counter before a diverse collection of bowls, measuring cups, spoons, cookbooks and a five-pound sack of masa, courtesy of Alice.

"You fixing to make you some hush puppies for supper?" asked Butch, hitching up his tool belt and consequently his work pants.

"Welcome to my culture, Butch. For mine is the world not of the hush puppy, but of the tortilla, kissing cousin to the hush puppy and the hoecake, possibly even to grits themselves."

"You're in a good mood, I can see."

"Butch, it turns out that I can teach. I can also probably garden. And I can certainly make tortillas."

"Yes 'um," said Butch. "I know you can do all of that and more. But what's this little silver gizmo here looks like a pancake griddle?"

"That's the tortilla press. You put the dough in here and mash it flat.

Alice sent me everything I need. I'll make a dozen or so extra so you can take them home to the missus."

"You ever done this kind of thing before, Miss Arden? No offense."

"Not exactly. But I'm sure it's no harder than writing a sonnet."

"Okay 'um. I'm just going on up and see to that dripping faucet in the upstairs bathroom. Couple of other things on the punch list, then we're out of here for true."

"That's good," she murmured absently, looking through one of the cookbooks. Page eight assured her, "Tortilla making is an art best learned at the knee of a Mexican grandmother." Well, she had a Mexican grandmother. Her credentials were in order. But she really didn't see any need for a press. Her grandmother had patted out the dough with her hands. Alice, bless her, was probably being overly cautious.

She added water to the masa, as directed, then stirred while the griddle heated. There was a rhythm to this. That's what she remembered. The patting sound had fallen into a cadence, kind of an iambic pentameter of the hands, which she now would emulate.

Somehow this dough was sticking tenaciously to her hands. She appeared to be wearing white gloves. She couldn't recall this happening to her grandmother. Ah, undoubtedly her grandmother dusted her hands with masa first.

Arden washed the glue-like film off her hands, dried them thoroughly, then dusted them well. Pat, pat, pat-a, pat, pat. The white gloves reappeared as if by magic.

Well, she would use the press after all. She washed her hands again, dusted the press, put in a wad of dough, and pressed it home. When she lifted the lid, the dough adhered evenly both to top and to bottom.

Were her cultural credentials in question here? She flung the press into hot soapy water, leaned against the counter and suppressed a growl.

On Miss Hattie's front porch across the field, her neighbor looked up from snapping her pole beans and waved. Arden straightened, took a deep breath and waved back.

Think. If the intuitive fails, try the reasoned. Reason told her she needed stick-free surfaces. Of course! Waxed paper! Between two sheets of waxed paper she rolled out the dough with a rolling pin. Ah, so far, so good. Now she'd coax off the top layer. It somehow seemed to resist, but only slightly. Patience here. This was a crucial, delicate step. But she'd only have to do the top layer this way.

Next she deftly flipped the tortilla over onto the waiting grill, and as it cooked she carefully pulled the other sheet of waxed paper away. This was working. A small stack of tortillas gradually collected on the blue plate.

When Butch came through with his ladder Arden invited him to taste. In fact, she would join him. Across the kitchen table from one another, a tall glass of milk before each, they buttered their tortillas.

"Well, ma'am," said Butch, still chewing.

"Don't say it. They taste like waxed paper. Damn!"

"I was fixin' to say, Miss Arden, that if your heart is dead set on tortillas tonight then you might just pick you up a dozen or so from the Menudo Palace. They don't close weekdays till three, and I think you could just about make it if you leave now."

"Menudo Palace? Here? In Midway? Where I live?"

"Between the dry cleaners and the food stamp store. You know, catty corner to the Unocal? We got a lot of migrant workers hereabouts."

"Butch, Butch," she said, reaching for her wallet and her keys, "what other reservoirs of knowledge are you keeping from me?"

By now Butch understood this was one of those questions Arden called *rhetorical*. No need to say back.

It was past four o'clock, and Arden could only describe herself using one of Butch's phrases, "happy as dead pig in the sunshine." José Martinez had stayed open just to save her life. For was he not from Morelia, the city of her grandfather? She had feasted on menudo, chiles rellenos, frijoles and flautas of a particular delicacy and flavor. Now, as José Martinez wrapped for her two dozen tortillas to go, a flyer on the counter next to her salsa-soaked check and ten dollar bill caught her eye.

"*Huelga*," it invited. "Support the strikers against Dixie Mushroom Farms. Friday, July 25 at 6 PM. In front of the IGA. *¡Hasta la victoria!*" She picked up the red flyer, tapped it with her finger. "*¿Qué pasa?*"

"*Esos gabachos*," he growled. "I got it up to here with them. *¿Sabe?* That's why I started this restaurant, so I wouldn't have to pick for them anymore. My brother, though, he stayed on. Did what they told him. Family growing up in one of those company shacks in the lane. He paid them rent too for this falling down house, and out of what? Nothing like a living wage did he earn. Then one day he's up on one of them ladders. They got mushrooms stacked up in flats, like skyscrapers. Too high. So he's up there working. *¿Comprende?* High as anything. You can't think how high. This ladder, it starts moving back and forth under him, back and forth, like he's *un hombre on zancos locos. Cómo se dice . . .*"

"Stilts?"

"*Exactamente*. So there he is up so high on that cheap old wooden ladder, no good for nothing, and he's trying to stay up but he can't. He tells me later it felt like he was coming down real slow, like his whole life was floating down with him, down until it smashes onto that slimy concrete.

"And his leg breaks in two places. The bone coming through. He's cut over the eye, shoulder out of its place. They drive him to the clinic, sure. They even pay the bill. But that's it for them. Next day they fire him because he can't work. He's no use to them anymore."

José Martinez shook his head and set the paper bag of tortillas on the counter. "He's got kids, a wife."

Arden picked up the sack, felt the warmth as if she were taking a human heart into her keeping. "*Hasta viernes, entonces*," she said, making for the door.

"*Momentito*," he said, "don't forget your change."

Chapter 31
Mars Trines Jupiter

When Vice President Wintermute telephoned late Saturday morning, the dean was in the bathtub reading *Time* magazine in a rare moment of peace and quiet. Bobbi June flung the door open on him suddenly, announced the call and tossed him a towel, part of which fell into his bath water.

She'd been acting funny for days. Spending more and more time with Benbow and Michaels out there at the old Faircloth place. Hen fests. Gab, gab, gab. Suddenly, as he toweled off and struggled into his terrycloth robe that said HIS over the heart, he had a vision of the three women, their mouths all going at once. What could they possibly find to say to each other?

And surely to God if something important did come up, she'd tell him. Surely by now she knew to do that.

He slipped across the linoleum floor toward the kitchen phone that Bobbi had left off the hook for him, took his place at the breakfast nook, noticed she hadn't taken away his plate yet. It still sat where he had left it, morning eggs turned to orange concrete on the Corelware.

"This is Kilgore," he said. "What can I do for you, sir?"

"Damn it, Kilgore, just what in hell is going on now with this Benbow case? I thought you and Hazard had put a lid on it. But now I open my morning paper and see this."

Kilgore glanced at the paper spread across the breakfast table, his eye falling on a picture of Richard Nixon schmoozing with some Chinese dignitary.

"Sir, I don't quite see . . ."

"The Midway paper, you idiot. Not the *Democrat*!"

The dean stretched his telephone cord, searching on his knees through the kitchen trash under the sink, until, yes, there it was under the egg shells and coffee grounds, Arden Benbow marching down High Road with a bunch of Mexicans carrying a banner saying "*Huelga.*" He let out a low moan.

"And that's only the half of it."

The dean huddled back into his breakfast nook, pulled his robe tighter across his chest, feeling a mortal chill. From the back bedroom he heard Bobbi June humming. She was sewing herself a dress for some damn party or other.

"What's the rest?" Kilgore asked.

"I went to the rugby game yesterday afternoon. Didn't happen to see you there."

Kilgore mumbled an excuse.

"At halftime," continued the vice president, "they gave a cheer. Our side, I'm talking about. And it wasn't the Midway Panthers cheer. No sir. They cheered some guy named Pindar."

"Pindar?"

" 'Pindar, Pindar, he's our man,' or some such. Hazard tells me he was some Greek athlete who wrote poetry on the side. I saw their T-shirts. You seen 'em yet?"

"No sir, I don't believe I have."

"Sometimes, Kilgore, I wonder if we're on the same planet. They show this blue guy doing a fairy leap in the air. You know those Greeks. Always into each other's pants."

"I don't believe they wore pants, sir."

"Damn it, Kilgore, you know what I mean. And I want it stopped."

"What stopped? I mean which part of it . . . sir?"

"The visibility part, I'm talking about. Don't make me do your job for you, Kilgore. I could start to like it."

Dean Kilgore found himself holding a dead phone. The vice president had never hung up on him before. Never called him an idiot before, either. Somewhere in the flatwoods of Billy Wayne Kilgore's mind, so far from the business center that he was hardly aware of it, something began to smolder. He knew only that his morning had been compromised and that the mowing would have to wait until late afternoon at best, if there was no rain, and there usually was.

He spent the remains of the morning whittling away at Bobbi June's long list of repairs, starting with a new hinge on one of the kitchen cupboards. Come lunchtime, Bobbi June was off somewhere selling real estate, and so he had to fix his own sandwich, but after that he watched some reruns from the winter Olympics and fell asleep in his La-Z-Boy during the bobsled races.

Chapter 32
Snapper

Three weeks later Billy Wayne sat in the breakfast nook finishing his coffee when Bobbi June carried a chair in from the dining room, put it under the kitchen cabinets, climbed up and started wrestling down the big coffee urn she used for church socials together with those big casserole things you burned candles under. She turned to see him watching.

"You don't want to know, Billy Wayne. Trust me."

Billy Wayne moaned. It had to be Benbow again. He just knew it. Sometimes, honest to God, he felt like he was in a roadrunner cartoon with Arden Benbow as the roadrunner and him as the coyote. Bobbi June carried the urn and the casserole dishes off somewhere, and was back home by the time he finished reading the Sunday paper. She washed up the dishes, put on a load of wash and then disappeared into her sewing room where from time to time he could hear her machine run and then the sound of her on the phone talking and laughing.

Billy Wayne was happy with his domestic life, but the sheer quiet and even simplicity of the morning made him vaguely mistrustful, as if that roadrunner might suddenly cross his path. But maybe not. Bobbi June always told him not to borrow trouble, that he should live in the moment, whatever that moment happened to be like.

Billy Wayne was never so much in the moment as when he was astride his Snapper 3000. The weather was fair, though afternoon thunderstorms had been predicted. Billy Wayne stuffed his feet into his Red Wings, grabbed his ball cap, and next thing he knew he was cutting wide, regular swaths through his summer grass. In fact Billy Wayne got as far as his favorite part, the easternmost hillock of his property, out there where nobody could possibly talk to him, when he made his first fatal mistake of the morning. He looked toward home.

And just as he did, the provost made a sharp turn off the highway and into Billy Wayne's driveway, almost taking out the mailbox. The man was wearing a suit and a tie in all this heat. Must have come from church, a place that Billy Wayne had vowed never to set foot in again, even if it cost him his job. He did have his limits.

The provost spotted Billy Wayne and waved his arm around wildly. Too late for Billy Wayne to pretend he didn't see him. He sighed and headed his Snapper back over to the carport and shut down the engine.

"You're a hard man to get hold of, Kilgore," complained Regis Factor, leaning against his ticking Mercedes and mopping his pink brow with a white handkerchief.

"It's summer," said the dean, dismounting, "and Sunday to boot."

"Your phone's been busy all morning. Can we go inside?"

"Must have been the missus," said Billy Wayne, levering off his Red Wings at the back door. Behind him, Factor sighed impatiently then followed him into the darkened utility room.

Bobbi June called from the adjoining kitchen, "Billy Wayne? That you?"

"Bidness, buttercup." She appeared, nodded, smiled at Factor, briefly inquired of his wife, then disappeared.

"A gem," observed Regis Factor. "A man's lucky to have a wife behind him, these days."

They both nodded solemnly. Billy Wayne led the provost into the family room, and they sat down on flowered chintz.

"It's Benbow again," said Factor.

"Wintermute told me a while back there was some trouble. I thought things might just die down on their own."

"That's the problem with you, Kilgore. You've got no initiative. Wintermute tells you there's a problem, and you decide to just wait for it to go away. You could have come to me, you know. That's what a team player would have done. Now I find out about the whole thing after the fact and by accident. When it's gotten worse."

"Worse?" said Billy Wayne, his sense of misery and dread deepening. "How could it be worse?"

"You know about the march a coupla three weeks ago, here in Midway?"

Billy Wayne nodded miserably. "It was in the local paper."

"Well, it didn't stop there, as you apparently hoped." He shot an icy glance at the dean. "She's in this thing up to her eyebrows and taken her students along for the ride. That's right. They're writing letters, passing out leaflets, giving speeches. They're going to march in Tallahassee next, and the scuttlebutt is that Benbow will lead the protesters right up the capitol steps."

Billy Wayne moaned.

"But that's not the worst of it. Oh, no. Here's the kicker. There's talk of the United Farmworkers stepping in."

The dean gave the provost a blank look.

"I'm talking Caesar Chávez and national media coverage, you idiot. Television. Prime time."

In the past month Billy Wayne had been called an idiot twice. Again he felt the burn of that little smoldering place somewhere inside him. "Now hold on just a minute there, Regis."

The provost abruptly rose and began pacing about. Finally he said, "I might have misspoken. We've got to hang together on this. If we let her get the upper hand here . . . Maybe, Billy Wayne, you don't entirely get the picture. The owner of Dixie Mushroom, the target of all this protest, is Dink Brasswell, a major contributor to Midway College and a former member of our board. There's money involved, man. Big money."

Billy Wayne reached absently for the pack of cigarettes he liked to carry in his breast pocket when he was working outside where Bobbi June couldn't see him. She had got him to quit smoking all right, but times like this it was hard. His fingertips caressed the now empty package, the feeling of lack helping him to recall the provost's breakfast back in May. He remembered Factor spearing the sausage off Billy Wayne's own plate, heard again the dull knife sawing, the fork tinging his plate afterward.

"So if you've got any ideas about how to handle Benbow, Kilgore, now's the time to put them on the table." Regis Factor sat down again.

Billy Wayne had to focus, use his mathematician's mind, the one that got him here in the first place. His job might be on the line. He had Bobbi June to think of. Real estate was well and good, but it could not provide for them in a steady way and let them live like they wanted to. No, he was the breadwinner here, and he must act like one.

"Well, Regis," he said, clearing his throat, "this is what I think. Now because Midway College is first and foremost a teaching institution, it behooves us to make sure our faculty do right by their students, without using questionable methods for questionable ends. Politics and pedagogy don't mix. They're oil and water. It seems to me we're well within our rights to look into those methods and aims and go from there. Providing, of course, that we're careful not to compromise her academic freedom."

"Academic freedom, my ass. She's untenured personnel, Kilgore. She doesn't have any goddamned academic freedom. Not until I say she does. But I see your point, in a way. This *is* about teaching, after all. The parents of these kids will make that clear as soon as they get mail about her lunatic ideas on teaching and start crawling up my butt. The responsible thing would just be to put an end to it right now. I can see that." He stood up from Bobbi June's chintz chair and held out his hand to her breadwinner. "I like it, Billy Wayne. I'm glad we had this little talk."

Billy Wayne shook his provost's hand warmly and led him to the front door. There still might be time left to finish the mowing after all, before those afternoon thunderstorms arrived. And yet, he thought, closing the door behind his superior, though he was no prude, he did somehow find all those allusions to posteriors vaguely unsettling.

He stood in the quiet foyer. No sound at all, not even his heart. When the silence had pressed on him long enough, he called out a little urgently, "Bobbi June, darling, where are you at anyhow?"

Chapter 33

Ruck

Bertha Michaels turned off the engine, glanced quickly into her rearview mirror, then repaired her lipstick. She would take her umbrella along just in case, though her own experience in personal disaster proved it was seldom accompanied by bad weather. Usually quite the opposite.

It was late on a Sunday afternoon, and glancing up she saw the Administration Building was dark except for a single light burning in the window of the chair's corner office where he waited for her. He had summoned her from Tallahassee to discuss problems with Arden Benbow's teaching. Somehow Bertha had become linked to Benbow, as if they were an aerial act flying perilously high above the heads of their colleagues. How had this happened?

She stepped out of her car into softening sunshine. Across the field, the ruggers in their bright jerseys pushed and shoved at one another, grunting obscurely. Her superior had left the main door unlocked, knowing she had no key. Inside the elevator she pushed five, recalled from her literary researches that the number five signified struggle and conflict. Other people were mowing their lawns right now, putting supper on the stove, washing their cars, dressing for the movies, while she, Bertha Michaels, must keep her appointment with struggle and conflict.

She stepped out on the fifth floor, tried to mute the sound of her heels resounding down the lonely polished surface of the corridor toward Dr. Hazard's office. His door stood open. As if he had not heard the hollow sound, he failed to look up from the sheaf of papers spread across his desk. She waited uncomfortably, then gave a tentative little knock on the door jamb. Without speaking, he motioned her into a side chair arranged to face not himself but instead his massive bookcases. She must turn her head at an odd angle before their eyes could meet. The high gloss and broad expanse of his rosewood desk stretched between them like mirage in a vast desert.

"Well?" he said finally, casting down his red pen.

"It's true," she said, "what you've heard about her teaching. But when she explains her reasons it seems to make sense."

The chair raised his eyebrows, waited.

"She says the way to teach our students is to give them something real to do, outside in the world, to create a situation where they must define for themselves the role of the poet and that that role is in some sense as working members of a real community. For example, there is the garden project in which the rugby team grows vegetables and distributes them to the community. Others, volunteers not even enrolled in Dr. Benbow's class, are transcribing the life histories of Midway's elderly population. Others are at work—"

"And that strikes you as a reasonable position to assume, Miss Michaels, in a department of English and with a student clientele known for their inability to obey even the simplest rules?"

Bertha knew this was not the real question. She knew something pressed upon this question, urging it into fatal bloom.

"I have had calls," her chair continued, "both from the provost and the dean regarding one of Miss Benbow's little projects. I refer to those members of her class who, we have recently learned, are teaching English to Dixie Farms agricultural workers and are now instigating them to riot over what they imagine to be unfair labor practices. Miss Michaels, our students arrive here politically naive and it is our job to see that they stay that way. Their parents expect that of us. Students are running around like mad dogs on half the campuses of this nation right now."

"Perhaps if you had not . . ."

"I am not of a mood to be criticized by you, Miss Michaels. I had hoped instead you might be of some assistance to me, to this department and to the very college itself. Dink Brasswell has sat on our board since before you, I believe, were hired at this institution. He has served us in untold ways, both professionally and—"

"Financially?" she guessed.

"Myriad way."

"The Mushroom Chair, sir?"

"Among other things, Miss Michaels, yes. Dixie Farms has fully funded that chair for more than three decades, providing a continuing bequest that enriches and elevates the quality of this faculty. Students come and they go, Miss Michaels. The faculty, most of them, at any rate, remain. The faculty is the backbone of any institution. If we don't protect our faculty, then I need hardly point out to you that Midway College, which now has a clear shot at the top ten among small, private liberal arts schools, will fall back, will be seen by the profession as having regressed into what it once was—a school for spoiled rich kids. None of us—am I correct in assuming this?—wants that, Miss Michaels."

A few minutes later, blinking in the late afternoon sunshine, she emerged like a moviegoer who had left a matinee, unsure what was shadow, what was substance. The lowing of a cow called her back to herself, reminded her to put one foot in front of the other, to reach into her bag for the car keys. Cries from the ruggers reached her as from a great distance. Then they chanted:

Ruck, maul, goal, scrum,
Pindar, Pindar, he's the one.

She paused at her car and breathed deep. The scent of cut grass suffused the air. And it had not rained. She tossed the umbrella into the backseat and turned the key in the ignition. It was then that she thought of it, what her mind had been laboring not so much to remember as to connect. Two things that belonged together but that time and strange intent had somehow separated. Turning the key had brought them together: Booth Hazard and the Mushroom Chair. For it was he who had occupied that chair for the past six or seven years. Yes, she was positive. And there had been, at the time of its being awarded, something of an outcry, as she recalled, over the possible irregularity of anyone functioning both as departmental administrator and holder of an endowed chair. Since then there had been only silence.

She released the emergency brake, threw the transmission into reverse, backed out past the chair's car, narrowly missing his right rear fender, then slipped it into drive, moving forward now, past the boys, the cows, toward the crossroads and the distant glow of Arden Benbow's kitchen.

"Arden, what is that over yonder?" Bobbi June stood on her friend's kitchen table, reaching high into the corner with her trim brush, trying to get the molding all nicely painted before Alice arrived on Tuesday.

"What's what?" asked Arden from her position under the kitchen sink where she worked on the drain trap.

"That little biddy black . . . oops! Arden, you got you a roach, honey. Quick, get it." She jumped down, whipped off one tennis shoe and nailed the insect just under the kitchen clock.

Arden was sitting on the floor, astonished. "Bobbi June," she said, "I think you've killed it."

"Of course I've killed it, sugar pie. You're in Florida now. It's kill or be killed." She scrubbed at the spot on the freshly painted wall with a detergent-soaked paper towel. "Nasty things."

Arden set down her wrench. "Bobbi June, you are very dear to me, but killing things violates my feelings. Such small creatures can't possibly eat much. Though come to think of it there do seem to be more of them than when I arrived."

"Nothing on this earth but rabbits multiplies any faster than cockroaches do. Believe me, it's not like you think, honey pot. You can't give them an inch. They're smart as little whips. You got to get Orkin out here first thing. Well, Monday anyhow. You don't want your Alice moving in here, right into a roach-infested house! That's no kind of welcome."

They heard a car pull up. Bobbi June looked through the kitchen window and called out, "Bertha, you come on in here now, gal, and tell Miss Arden all about roaches and their ways." Then she turned back to Arden, still stunned on the floor, a wrench cradled in her lap. "She'll tell you. After thirty years, this is a woman who knows her roaches."

Five minutes later they were both on their knees, one on either side of Bertha's chair, chaffing their friend's hands.

"Darlin' girl," said Bobbi June, "what can be the matter? Why I haven't seen color like that since Billy Wayne's cousin Emory got bit by a coral snake and almost died."

"It's the chair," said Bertha, bursting into tears. "No, it's more than that." She looked at Bobbi June.

"Well, what is it? Lord have mercy, if you don't unburden yourself then we might as well start out right now for the emergency room in Tallahassee."

"Is it me, Bertha? Have I got you in trouble?" asked Arden. "What can I do?"

"Oh, it's not you," sobbed Bertha. "Not you, dear child, it's me. They've used me, and I've let them. I will give you one last message, on your behalf, not theirs, and then have no more to do with their machinations."

"Are those boys being bad again, darlin'?"

"What message, Bertha? Is it about my involvement with the farm workers?"

"Ostensibly," she sniffed. Bobbi June handed her a box of tissues and patted her hand. "He says you are to sever your connections with the farm workers immediately and to consider all of your teaching methods under the severest scrutiny."

"Oh land," breathed Bobbi June, sinking down onto the floor next to Bertha's chair. "Arden, you've got to trim your sails, sugar pie. I can't tell you how many women faculty have come and gone since I've been here. I'll say time and again to Billy Wayne, 'Now, whatever happened to that nice new woman in biology? You know the one. I like her,' and he just says she didn't make the cut. Happens time after time. And you're not going to make the cut either, honey pot, if you don't do what they say. Or at least pretend to. You've got no choice."

Arden looked at Bertha, who sniffed, and nodded, and suppressed a final sob.

Chapter 34
Pride & Prejudice

Arden crawled on her hands and knees through the cabbages, under a waning moon. It had to be around here somewhere, that cursed book. She could swear it contained a whole chapter on trimming one's sails. Why had she flung it through the window that night? She couldn't remember. But now her life depended on finding it. Ah yes, her hand had struck something. She shone her flashlight. Yes, it was the book, mud-encrusted, with bits of straw and compost clinging to it.

Had she heard the thump of Miss Hattie's cane on her porch? The light from her neighbor's living room window cast a triangular patch outside on the ground. Her neighbor's front door closed. It must be ten o'clock. Late for Miss Hattie.

She picked up the book and made her way through her sleeping house. Compromise. Both her friends had counseled her to compromise, cut back, get small, hush herself for the sake of tenure.

She took the stairs, two at a time. Weeks of reading this book in bed and it now seemed necessary to be in bed to read it. Creature of habit that she was! She ripped off her clothes, quickly performed her ablutions, struggled into her pajamas and took her place on the mattress.

In the novel of manners there can be no resolution without compromise. Transfixed as the heroine has been between two polarities—those of self and society—she can only gain validation and membership by virtue of her stately, generous acquiescence.

Arden was not going to sleep again, not in this lifetime. Only a turn in the garden, several turns, would calm her mind. She snatched her jeans down from the hook in the closet, stepped into them and pulled them up, tucking her pajamas in and zipping. In the mirror over her dresser she caught a glimpse of herself, harried and wild-eyed. Did Elizabeth Bennett ever look like this? More important, did Elizabeth Bennett ever have a wife and six children to support?

Halfway down the staircase she paused. This house, she thought, running her hand along the worn banister. Shelter. Alice had given notice at work, would be here soon with the rest of the children. They would all be evicted unceremoniously at the crossroads, their belongings stacked around them. What had she been thinking!

She directed her feet to the garden. Gardens, she corrected. Crossroads Gardens. Six raised beds filled with good things to eat. Health. Those green leaves. How could she leave them? She bent down close, brought her nose into the heart of the kale. "You're beautiful," she said aloud.

"What you doin', Miss Arden, out here in the dark talkin' to them vegetables? Folks gone think you crazy for sure. Lock you up."

"Miss Hattic. I thought you were asleep."

"I almost was. I hear you goin' in and comin' out, comin' out, goin' in. I hear you out here, thinkin' so loud you might wake up the dead. Now tell me, what's goin' to ease your mind, child?"

Arden looked up at the sky so tears would not run down her face. "I have injured a friend. And I might be fired and lose my house, and Alice has quit her job and is coming three thousand miles, and all of this, every bit of it, is my own damned fault."

"Trouble's here," said Miss Hattie. "He's back. Can Miss Hattie help any?"

"You could, if you wouldn't mind."

"Mind! It was you," she said, "run over that time fat jump out of the pan, set my kitchen on fire. It was you put it out and never said nothing 'bout it to nobody. It was you sent over and ask about the garden and the young mens and them learning all about how to live in this world so's it don't cost but instead makes bounty for the Lord and his children. It was you give me a place to go most days and more good things out of that garden than even I needed or could think to want. All that. Now tell me, what can I do."

"Would you stay here, at my house, while I go talk to Lupe? The kids are asleep."

"This about the march next week?"

"That's right. The college doesn't want me or the students there."

"Hard to see it happening without you and them. Y'all been with it since the get-go. 'Course if I can find somebody to carry me to Tallahassee, I'll go. Got no college mens telling me do this and not do that. Seems like a education ought to be about more than telling folks what not to do. Well, you get on along now and see what does Lupe say. I'll just go sit inside and watch that fine TV y'all have got you, where everybody look most as big as they own size. Nothing wrong with that."

Minutes later, Arden slipped her jacket off the peg in the hall and rolled the Harley out of the shed. It must be close to eleven, but Lupe was most likely up, getting the last of the flyers addressed. She kick-started the bike and soon was roaring toward the lanes.

Ah, she had forgotten her helmet and the air stirred her hair, her spirit, her headlight searched through forest mists into future time. What should she do? It hurt her pride to back down. It hurt her pride to be this vain. Her throat tightened against the anger, the disappointment. She wanted to be bigger than she really was.

She turned off the hard road and onto the soft dirt of the lane, then slowed, moving as quietly as possible through a tunnel of lacy pepper trees.

Lights were out in most of the cabins. Cars, like sleeping dogs, pulled up close. Toys left out in the dirt, relics of the spent day. Before Lupe's place she killed the engine and rocked the Harley back on its stand. Looked up into the clear night, the watching stars.

There were a few cars at Lupe's, parked in the rectangles of light from the window. She heard voices, knew herself about to intrude into lives already troubled. And what was she coming to do? It was as if she carried a message she herself has not been permitted to read. Arden Benbow, indecision's own personal courier.

At the door, she knocked softly. In a moment, Grace, the shy literacy volunteer, opened it slightly, then seeing Arden, flung it wide. Several women worked at a card table beneath a suspended bulb, addressing flyers for the march. Eugene, one of the ruggers, stood at the sink washing up the dishes. Lupe crossed the room, smiling in welcome. When her hand slipped into Arden's, time slowed and sensation deepened, grew acute, accurate. Arden recorded the warm, rough feel of Lupe's hand, memorized contours embossed by work harder than her own.

In a cabin like this one, close as the chambers of her own heart, José Martinez's brother must lie sleepless with pain.

With deliberate ease she picked up a folding chair from against the wall and opened it out at the table. "Sorry I'm late," she said to everyone and to no one. Then she sat down at the card table and pulled a stack of leaflets toward her.

Chapter 35
Loose Maul

Bertha Michaels had never been to a rugby match before. She sat in her car waiting for Arden, but soon heat shimmered off the dash, and she began to regret having come at all. Why was she here? The clear boundaries that used to separate her private from her professional life had grown indistinct in her mind.

In a moment she heard a motorcycle rumbling, turned her head, and there she was, Arden Benbow, with her two children squeezed into a sidecar. She cut the engine and waved. They all removed helmets, and then when Bertha stepped out of her car, they surrounded her, leading her into the bleachers.

Jamie had brought along a shopping bag full of popcorn, and Kip bought Cokes at the concession stand for everybody. Arden kept waving to the boys on the field, and they raised clenched fists back in what she supposed was some kind of obscure sports gesture. Rugby, it would appear, was a foreign language. She accepted popcorn from Jamie.

Just as she began to relax a little, she noticed the president and his wife sitting down below them. She straightened. For President Cager had been at the march in Tallahassee yesterday morning. Whether by accident or design she couldn't say. But there, nevertheless. She had seen him bear witness to the spectacle of Assistant Professor Arden Benbow marching up the Appalachee Parkway toward the capitol at the head of the parade, holding aloft a red flag with a black eagle rippling on the morning air.

Perhaps he had not recognized his new faculty member. Perhaps none of their other colleagues had attended. Aside from Arden's invitation to the game, Bertha's phone had not rung all day.

And yet she knew discovery was just a matter of time. She would be found guilty of collusion with the enemy. Her golden epaulets would be summarily removed from her tunic and her sword broken.

Strangely enough it didn't seem to matter very much. She would accept this matchless, bright day as the gift that it was. After all, she had come to the game, the rugby game. With her friends. On her own time. She gestured to the hotdog vendor, holding up four fingers.

In a moment the two teams lined up and tried to push each other over, apparently. Fans yelled: piggy, piggy, piggy. Everybody on the field fell down, and then they got up and did it all over again. Bertha Michaels munched on her hotdog, feeling very much like Margaret Mead at some primordial, inchoate celebration.

Then somebody fumbled the strangely shaped ball and away they all went, scrambling about, yelling ruck, ruck, ruck. Midway recovered, and a student across the field blared a trumpet in triumph. Then Arden stood on a bench and yelled, "Do it for Pindar, rugby boys! ¡Hasta la victoria!"

The president looked straight in the direction of Assistant Professor Arden Benbow, who was waving her clenched fist. Bertha followed his eyes as they traveled from Benbow to herself, Full Professor Bertha Michaels, assistant chair of English, sporting an incriminating trail of mustard down the front of her blouse.

The next day Bertha leaned forward in a white lawn chair under the dappled shade of an ancient pear tree at Crossroads Gardens. She may have spotted a blue heron. It must have wandered off course somehow.

Extraordinary. She brought her binoculars to bear, and yes, it definitely was a blue heron. So stately a bird. Color contained, and the more beautiful for that. It stood in a patch of grass, out of context, yet regal, creating its own context. Then she caught a glimpse of something more flamboyant. A tuft of crimson on the back porch. Ah, Kip, the eldest son, bringing her a mug of coffee. She tousled his red hair, thanked him, sank back into the commodious chair. Sunday morning.

Odd how peaceful she could feel, knowing with certainty that her career in academe was over, the striving part, at any rate. The rosewood desk, the delicate Spode teacup would never be hers. Perhaps she had known it all along, but never quite so plainly or dramatically as yesterday when the mustard had cascaded down onto her silk blouse.

She sipped her coffee and thought of nothing. For the moment. Then her mind engaged again, began to plan. She would sell her condominium in Sun City, perhaps buy a little place on the Sopchoppy River, live simply.

She heard the heron flapping leathern wing, watched her circle and pass overhead, then disappear toward distant marshes.

The day after tomorrow Alice would arrive with the rest of the children. The house resounded with last minute hammering and an occasional shout. Then Bertha heard a strange roaring at the front of the house, and now, around the corner lurched and plunged a large, flatbed truck piled high with bales of pine straw, driven by a woman. Patches of pink defined her cheeks. For a moment, Bertha thought, unaccountably: Health is coming for me.

She rose, approached in curiosity. The woman set the brake, killed the engine, then leaped out almost on top of Bertha.

"Boss Granny," she said, hand extended. "Full Court Press. Brought Arden some pine straw for her garden. Don't know why. That woman has managed to wrangle more damn donated goods from me for her harebrained poetic projects. Who the hell are you?"

"Bertha Michaels."

"You're not a writer, are you? I could use some good sex. Fiction, I meant. No offense, I meant fiction, of course." Boss Granny blushed. "There's no harm in me. Arden will tell you that."

Bertha blushed too, said she was Arden's colleague at Midway College—for the time being, anyway—then invited Boss Granny to join her under the pear tree.

"Bunch of wild animals out at that college, you ask me. Never had much use for academics, personally. Present company excepted, of course. Arden too. But I prefer to work for a living. Speaking of which, I'll just unload this pine straw for the garden and be on my way."

"Must you?"

"Say," said Boss Granny, peering thoughtfully into Bertha's eyes. "You're not married or anything. Are you?"

"I'm perfectly free," she said with some surprise. "Yes I am."

"Charmed," said Boss Granny.

Arden came up to see them both flushed with delight. She hugged Boss Granny, and soon all three of them were pitching pine straw from the truck into the vegetable beds and spreading it into little nests. Afterward they set out the irrigation hoses and retreated to their chairs under the shady branches where they listened to miniature rivers coursing from plant to plant under coverings of pine straw.

Boss Granny seemed strangely quiet. She looked at her big feet in their scuffed high tops, then over at Bertha. "Hot," she said, taking off her ball cap and fanning herself with it. "But I'm glad to be here with you two lovely ladies today."

"I do believe I'll make us all some lemonade," said Bertha, rising as if in a dream. "That is, if you can stay."

"Oh yes, thank you, Miss Michaels. I mean, Dr. Michaels."

"Bertha, by all means."

"Well, Bertha. That'd be more than lovely," said Boss Granny, blushing again.

Chapter 36
Aztlán

"Oh," said Alice, speechless before the spectacle of her Mexican bathtub. "It's yellow!" Behind the Jacuzzi, delicate arches framed the light. Jamie had painted hanging baskets with purple wisteria trailing about. Alice turned slowly, taking in the room. Butch, Altron and Arden studied her reaction with delight, then raced back to unload the bags from the hearse.

Alice walked alone through the lovely, high-ceilinged rooms, wandering at last into a room freshly painted from the wainscoting up in a blue that lightened magically as it rose toward the ceiling. Her desk and music stand stood on either side of a window. This room was hers. The music room.

She heard Hillary, Max, Ellen and Arthur pounding upstairs to the second floor, then calling down gleefully from the attic rooms. Kip, Jamie and Arden guided, identified, explained. The house rang with laughter. In a moment she felt strong arms encircling her, her head tipping back, her mouth losing itself in homecoming.

The hush from the hall meant there were children out there, waiting. Their arms around each other, she and Arden led them out onto the porch, into the yard, down the paths between the flourishing gardens. Alice plucked a cabbage blossom, tucked it behind her ear. Young people in brightly colored rubber boots stood in the beds, weeding, turning the earth. Others sat under trees, reading aloud to each other or writing in notebooks.

Seated in a rocking chair, wearing a straw hat, sat an old black woman in a pale blue dress, gesturing with her cane at a thick-necked white boy with a pruning saw in his hand. Then she noticed Alice, smiled, said, "Well, we been waitin' on you. And some of us not too patient at that." Then she laughed and thumped her cane three times.

Several days later, when Alice was in her music room practicing her cornet, she heard a tapping on the front screen door. A black boy of thirteen or so waited in T-shirt and cutoffs.

"I be King David. Y'all's yard man."

"I didn't know we had a yard man, to tell you the truth, King David. Does Arden know about this?"

"No ma'am. She don't. Her boy Kip tell me to ax you. Say he got two mamas or some such."

"The young men and women from the college take care of the gardens."

"Yes ma'am, but look here at this mess you callin' a yard. I clean all this up good. A little mowin' and edgin' and you be in bidness. I got the tools. I can get 'em. Plant you some flowers up here around the house." He gestured with a graceful hand. "Make it look real nice for you."

"Well, King David, you certainly are a persuasive business man."

"Yes ma'am, I am that. And I work cheap. Miss Hattie can vouch for me. She know my mother an all."

"Tell you what, King David. Let me check this out with everybody, because that's how we do things around here. Come back about this time tomorrow. With any luck, you and I will both have jobs by then."

Chapter 37
Musical Chairs

When Bobbi June got home from work that same day, Billy Wayne was sitting at the dinner table holding his head in his hands. That just about tore it for her. "Billy Wayne," she said, "you may not realize it but you are perfectly capable of starting dinner your own self. I have a career to worry about same as you."

"It's not that," he moaned through clenched hands.

"Well what is it, sugar? Tell mama."

"It's the Mushroom Chair," he told her, suddenly looking up. "We lost it."

She had expected those little tight tears of frustration that he let her see sometimes, but his eyes were dry. This must be the worst kind of misery and him trying like sixty to stuff it down inside, like he always did.

"Billy Wayne, you're going to give yourself a stroke. Now just turn loose of it, right here, right now, sugar pie. Spread it out all over this table, right here"—she thumped it for emphasis, the exact spot—"and then we'll make sense out of it. Now just what do you mean, honey lamb, by the mushroom chair? How can there be such a thing on this earth as a mushroom chair?"

"Brasswell," he choked out. "He settled with the strikers."

"Well, darlin', that's just wonderful. Now we can eat mushrooms again and the people can go back to work and Arden will save herself a whole lot of time and energy that she's been spending on this. And a lot of other people too. But what do you mean about a chair made out of mushrooms, and if you ever had it, how could you lose it?"

"You are not understanding me," he said through clenched teeth.

"Well no, I guess I am not, Billy Wayne. I am trying, but I am not succeeding. Now you just be a little kinder to yourself and you might find out I am not some stupid mistake you made as a young man. I am a Lumley, born and bred, and I know how, believe me, I know how, to deal with trouble. If that's what this is."

"The Mushroom Chair is an endowed position presently occupied by Booth Hazard."

"Well now, honey, let me interrupt you one little minute. Now Booth is the chair of English."

Billy Wayne nodded agreement.

"How can he possibly be the English chair and the Mushroom Chair at the same time? That doesn't make good sense, Billy Wayne. How many chairs can you sit in at once?" She almost laughed but caught herself.

"Ordinarily you can't. It's against our bylaws. An exception was made. I don't know, years ago. Honey, I can't explain it. The point is he had it, the Mushroom Chair. And now he doesn't. It no longer exists. Brasswell, out at Dixie Farms, knows who he's got to thank for all that uproar over their labor relations with the Mexicans. Arden Benbow is who. And when he had to give in to the union, he just decided he couldn't afford being generous to Midway College any more. And I don't blame him. She shouldn't have messed around in things that don't concern her."

"Arden says injustice is everybody's concern. Besides, sugar, these are her people who are falling off ladders, slipping and falling, getting hurt and then getting fired because they're hurt."

"I don't give a damn what Arden Benbow says or doesn't say. Do you understand that? I've got a college to run here. I'm respected. I've got a position to protect."

"Are they blaming you, darlin', about this Mushroom Chair?"

"They will," he groaned. "Oh they will. The president will squeeze the vice president, who will squeeze the provost, who will squeeze me."

"And Hazard will squeeze you too?"

"Oh, most assuredly. Him worst of all. Now that he's lost his damn chair, he'll be shopping for a deanship to take up the slack. I know him."

"Well, Billy Wayne, seems to me like you've just got to get him another chair."

"An *endowed* chair. Not just any damn chair. We're talking money here, not furniture. Do you understand me, B. J., honey? Something of great worth. That's what endowed means."

"I know what *endowed* means, Billy Wayne. There was a time when I myself have been described as endowed, though that fact may have escaped your notice lately, busy as you as you have been with what you call your career. You may not have noticed, too, that I myself am no stranger to laying my hands on cash from time to time. So when I tell you we've got to find us another chair, why that's exactly what I mean. Sugar pie."

Chapter 38
The Way of the World

Bertha Michaels, who had never in her life wanted a family, found herself in the back seat of a hearse with seven children. This was a family celebration. A tin shovel stuck into the small of her back. She removed it and handed it to the daughter named Ellen. They were all just starting out for St. George Island, where they would spend the day sunning, swimming, exploring, kite flying and eating the basket of food Arden and Alice had prepared.

Everyone was here except their dear friend Mr. Topaz Wilson, who had returned from California last week. He was in town today seeing about a job with the Florida State dance department. Strange, thought Bertha, how she had been so set on retiring in California, and now, it seemed, California had come to her. Maybe that was how things worked. Certainly when Arden moved here from California she believed she was leaving her culture behind, and then it turned out she was part of a Mexican community, right here in Florida. Aztlán, she called it.

And somehow she, Bertha Michaels, had become an honored guest of Aztlán and no longer a secret agent in the employ of academe.

Unless, she thought with amusement as they started over the Panacea Bridge, she was a double agent. Only last week, well after the union contract had been negotiated and things seemed to be settling down, the chair had once again called her in and asked her what she knew about Crossroads Gardens. "For, Miss Michaels," he had warned, "I have begun to suspect an irregularity."

"I think, sir, her pedagogical methods are innovative rather than irregular. She teaches them poetry through gardening, sir. I've explained all that. It's basically a theory of organicism. Art is alive, she says. There's no difference between writing a poem and raising a tomato. If you can do one, then you can do the other."

"Yes, yes, I've heard all that romantic claptrap before, Michaels. What I'm asking you, what I want to know now is really quite simple. Can you tell me, Miss Michaels, precisely where all that produce goes? Because if she's using student labor to line her own pockets . . . There ought to be . . . there certainly are laws against something like that."

"Oh no, sir, it's nothing like that. Rest assured. They've taken very special care. One of the young men, Eugene, the right wingback, I believe, is in accounting and another, one of the halfbacks, as I recall, is in pre-law. Michael Rosen is his name. And they've set up complete and detailed books. Most of the food goes to Midway senior citizens or residents who are on food stamps, or to agricultural workers, because Dixie Farms still pays them quite poorly, notwithstanding the new contract. From whatever food is sold, five percent goes to Miss Hattie, their technical advisor, and five percent goes to Crossroads Gardens Cooperative for operating expenses. One way or another, ninety percent of whatever is produced goes to people in the community, a more stellar performance than most major charities, I believe, sir."

She never would forget his face.

Her reverie was interrupted by Arden, checking on her from the front seat. "How're you doing, Bertha?"

"Splendid," Bertha called back. "We're all just splendid."

Chapter 39

Witnessing

Booth Hazard's black Mercedes rolled and pitched over the dirt road, laboring toward Arden Benbow's End of Summer Party. His wife's eyes bore into the side of his head. She disliked unpaved roads and didn't much like his colleagues either. Cars lined both sides of the road and he could find no place to park. Then—my God!—it was Bertha Michaels, wearing dungarees and waving cars up onto Benbow's property, like a common parking lot attendant at a country fair!

She motioned him into a place at the end of a long line of cars. He waited outside his dusty car, while inside his wife attended to her face. Dust, he mused, staring down at his formerly glossy shoes, the primordial image for mutability and death. Long ago he had drafted an article called "Dust Imagery in Eliot's *Wasteland*." Probably should revise it and ship it out. Maybe put a colon in that title somewhere first, for weight.

He'd deal with Michaels later. He found he could no longer trust her. That was why he'd had to come here himself, to see just exactly what was going on. His wife took his arm and struggled over ruts in her patent leather pumps, glaring up at him accusingly. The invitation to Benbow's party had said casual dress, but what other people chose to call casual, Booth Hazard and his wife knew to be inappropriate.

The late afternoon light all around them glowed strangely, the way it sometimes did during tornado watches. Streaks of pink and red mottled the west, like blood poisoning. He felt a sudden gust of wind, heard a snapping sound. Next to the front porch stood a flagpole with a huge flag floating to rest like a woman's skirt, then billowing open again suddenly, like a red poppy blooming in a time exposure shot. That was when he spied its emblem, a menacing black bird, wings outstretched, on a field of deep red. A guerrilla flag, it looked like, flying over the old Faircloth Plantation as if over a foreign country.

He had seen this flag before, somewhere else. Now he remembered, remembered the newspaper photo Wintermute had shoved before his eyes that miserable morning a couple of weeks back. The photo of Arden Benbow and the United Farmworkers and half of Tallahassee marching on the capitol, a scene witnessed, unfortunately, by the president himself.

Wintermute had called him in, shut the door. "You listen here," he had said, jabbing the rolled up newspaper into Hazard's tie, "you've left me looking like a supreme asshole to the president. You've got to handle this situation, and do it fast. This problem is on your watch, Hazard. Now do whatever it takes and do it yesterday."

"But what about Kilgore?"

"Factor delegated to Kilgore, and Kilgore delegated to you. That's how it works. You know that."

"But Kilgore said—"

"Kilgore doesn't exist. Get that straight. He's out of the loop. Always has been. The man's a teacher, not an administrator. You work things right, Hazard, and you could be in line for that opening. On the fast track. Work them wrong and you might find yourself back in the classroom right alongside our friend Billy Wayne."

And before he had a chance to demonstrate to the vice president that Booth Hazard was not another Kilgore, Brasswell had capitulated, signed a union contract. With a stroke of the pen that man had deprived him of his endowed chair, his promised deanship and the reputation he had spent a lifetime shaping.

Not that he was throwing in the towel. No, but he knew he had to go it alone now. Understood by no one, helped by no one. He saw himself parachuting into enemy territory, dropping to his knees, cutting free his chute and crawling forward under heavy enemy fire to set up his radio on a distant mountaintop.

Actually, the extended metaphor collapsed under him now, for communication was no longer an option. He couldn't even discuss this with his own wife, who stood now, admiring, to judge from her expression, this very flag that symbolized his undoing.

He noticed Helen Core tugging unpleasantly on his suit jacket and directing him and his wife around the side of the house. He had been right to put that woman out to pasture long ago. She was about to become an embarrassment. At least he had handled *that* right.

Behind the house a crowd of people stood talking and laughing, balancing paper plates, a mixed bunch from both town and gown. Most of them Mexicans, farm workers, probably, the very people in question. He recognized Butch Quickle, who had built their deck last summer. A thick young man in a brown cowboy hat looked familiar and when he removed it momentarily, revealing black, slicked-back hair, Hazard suspected he was his own exterminator, here as a guest.

Ruggers were setting up a makeshift stage and putting in place folding chairs and coolers filled with ice. He saw that tall, effeminate black man Benbow arrived with in the first place, the one they had all thought was her husband, until things got worse and worse. He was waving his arm around, directing the rugby boys in their work. As if he belonged here.

Things seemed ready to begin. People sitting down. Then the black man jumped up on stage and set up a music stand and two plastic chairs. The red-haired boy and a middle-aged woman seated themselves and begin playing a cornet duet.

"That's my wife," said Benbow, appearing suddenly at his left elbow, "with our son."

Then a red-haired teenage girl and a black boy got up, and they had a basket filled with flowers, which they presented to the mayor of Midway, amidst much clapping. A woman from the literacy program awarded a plaque to a student inappropriately named Grace for her work teaching agricultural workers to read English. A Mexican woman handed Arden a bunch of wildflowers, weeds really. Then dark men in white shirts leaped up on the stage and played trumpets and guitars wildly and off-key. They wore heavy black wool outfits and perspired visibly, mopping their brows with handkerchiefs between numbers, all of which sounded alike.

The wind died down, and the pink and yellow faded out of the sky. Porch lights and a few flaming torches dotted the night. Mosquitoes dive-bombed Hazard's neck. He needed a drink, had eaten nothing all day. His eye wandered to a collection of ice chests, from which people were helping themselves. He felt a flicker of interest, almost excitement. Benbow was perhaps serving alcohol to minors. For him, opportunity often came like this, without planning, opening before him as if by cosmic consent.

He approached a green ice chest and flipped it open. In a sea of ice, dark bottles bobbed. He lifted one close for inspection. Root beer!

The black boy from before came up to him and stood silently, then flipped open the red chest next to the green, saying, "We got Co-Cola over here, you want that. Or RC on down the line. I'm King David, the yard man here."

Hazard could not answer. He simply stood, looking about him.

His wife reached into one of the ice chest and took the cap off a Coke, then handed the bottle to him, inquiring, "Booth, are you all right?" He nodded, stood, sipping the soft drink absently. Another child with red hair, a girl, came up to the black boy and stood at his side, listening to the music. Hazard's wife bent down and said to her, "My, all you children must look just like your daddy."

"No," she replied, "we all look just exactly like ourselves."

Then the musicians filed off the stage, and a man who seemed to be some kind of construction worker climbed up in dusty white bib over-alls and ponytail and read some doggerel about rugby, sheetrock and assorted vegetables. Tattoos snaked down both his arms.

The captain of the rugby team now leapt up on the stage and thanked the tattooed man for teaching them all "the manly art of poetry." Pindar was mentioned with reverence, though not Whitman, Hazard was relieved to notice. Afterward there was much sentimental hugging and displays of emotion among the team members, who by now were also on stage milling about. Finally the captain invited every-one to share in the rich harvest, and there followed a mad rush for food set out on unstable trestle tables.

Booth Hazard felt as if he was coming down with something. He felt it moving along his veins and arteries, a cramping throughout his gastrointestinal tract. He wanted to leave this party. There was no place for him here. He might as well be from outer space. He was leaving. No question. But when he looked around for his wife, he found her standing in line with a paper plate and accepting a huge spoonful of fried okra, another of some orange ethnic food and a cob of corn from Bertha Michaels herself.

And then it happened, what he had been waiting for all this time. A young blond lady named Shannon, a former work-study student of his, asked if she might have a word with him. In private. Under an ancient oak, beyond all light from the house, she spoke the words he had been waiting to hear. Waiting, it seemed, all of his life. Marijuana. Marijuana growing at the back of Miss Benbow's property. A whole field of it. Higher than her shoulder. As a Christian, she said, she knew she just had to tell someone in authority.

"My dear," he assured her, "you have done as Christ would have wished."

Chapter 40
Borderlands/La Frontera

Late afternoon contemplated yielding herself to the gentle advances of evening. Cicadas tuned up. Arden had miscalculated the remaining light as she replaced the Harley's spark plugs the day after her End of Summer Party. Somehow she could see far but not near, could see Hattie's chair on her front porch, but not the respective sizes of the wrenches at her own left toe. Could the lenses in her fine eyes be thickening, their action slowing? Would she soon require tortoise shell glasses hanging on a little gold chain around her neck? Coatlicue, goddess of transformation, she said to the dimming light, are you come for me?

Damn. She raised up on her elbows seeking out, as was her habit, the comforting shape of Hattie in her watching chair. But something in her neighbor's body language alerted her. Next thing Arden knew a car door slammed, and she saw the sheriff making his way up the walk toward the front porch, moving his bulk along faster than she would have thought possible. She hailed him from the garage, and he flicked on the beam of his flashlight and shone it in her eyes momentarily, then killed it.

"We got us a world of trouble, Miss Arden," he told her, coming close, his breath rasping. "I got something I need to show you."

He took her by the arm, and they walked fast together across the open field, beyond the glow of household light, then into the darkening woods where the underbrush grew thick. Cat's claws tore at their clothes. They veered around poison ivy, brushed mosquitoes away, moving to the pulse of crickets and frogs. Finally they stood in a clearing.

"Now," the sheriff said, directing his beam toward a tall, healthy crop. "Do you know what that is?"

Arden felt a little annoyed. "Certainly I know what that is, Sheriff. It's our celery."

He stood transfixed, tipped his white hat back on his head, said at last, "Well now, ma'am."

Arden decided to pick up the burden of failed conversation. "It's Eugene's baby, really. He's trying out celery here in this low-lying area. As an agricultural experiment."

"And just who in hell is Eugene?"

"Eugene is a poet," she said. "And a particularly fine right wing-back."

"And a con artist. Also particularly fine. What you've got growing here is a field of prime mary ju-ana. Best I've seen in a long, long time."

"Really?"

He unclipped a walkie-talkie from his shirtfront and mumbled numbers into it so fast she couldn't tell what he was saying.

"What's going to happen to Eugene?" Arden asked when he finished.

"You can save your breath worrying about Eugene. Folks out at the college been protecting college boys since the founding. They're experts at it, you might say. Bad boys is their cash crop. No, Miss Arden, the question is not what's going to happen to Eugene. It's what's going to happen to you?"

~

Hattie White was right there on her front porch when Arden and the sheriff came out of the woods. She hailed him by his first name. "Halston. You, Halston. You get on over here."

"Police bidness, Miss Hattie. Can't stop for nothing."

"I'm talking police bidness. Now you get yourself on over here."

They came up on her porch.

"You in my world now. You sit down, now, hear? I got material evidence, I do. Miss Arden ain't planted no drugs."

"I know that, Miss Hattie," he said, resting one buttocks cheek uneasily on her porch railing, "but the crop's on her land and that makes her an accessory after the fact. I'm going to have to book her. No way around it."

"Ain't she been sending greens to your granny all summer long?"

"Well, yes 'um. But the law's the law."

"I'm coming around to talking law, Halston. That little bit a land way back there that lays so low seems like it ain't good for much of nothing?"

He nodded.

"Well, sir, that's *my* land, sorry as it is. That carpetbagger lived here before me?"

"That'd be Mr. Gifford. Giles Gifford, if memory serves."

"He the one. Mr. Gifford, he's fixin' to fence off his plantation. Sets out little biddy yellow flags all over tarnation. This mine, little yellow flags say. Well, sir, I tell him that land over there be mine. Been in my family since the war, like Mrs. Faircloth want. No sir, he say, it be mine. Legal. I go to court with him. Nice girl from Legal Aid, she help me out. By the time it's all over with, I got me the papers to say that sorry piece of land belong to me and my heirs, Hattie White, free and clear.

"So now I reckon if you be needin' an accessory after any facts you can think of, Mr. Halston, then you better lock me up instead. I'm ready." She held out her wrists.

"Now Miss Hattie, ain't no call to get yourself exercised about all this."

"I got the papers, Halston Crawford, to prove what I'm sayin'. In a tin box down to the bank. Don't you think I ain't."

"Well, how about we all just sleep on this for now. I'm sure this whole thing's just some kind of misunderstandin'." He groaned to his feet. "Whee dog, I'm beat, I can tell you. This has been one hell of a day."

They watched him lumber off toward the sheriff's car, saw the white machine leap alive and wheel on out of their lives.

Chapter 41
Full Court Press

"Just tell him it's the CEO of Full Court Press and that he better lock up the family silver," Boss Granny told President Cager's astonished secretary. "And Billy Wayne here, he's my accomplice. Tell him we've got an offer he'd be crazy to refuse. Tell him it's about a chair, and it's about money to buy it with. Tell him I'm serious as a heart attack. Tell him whatever comes to your mind, honey, but be quick about it. I've got a business to run even if you don't."

In a moment they were seated before a balding man behind a big desk. But he moved around it to shake their hands and seat them. He was tall and self-assured, like Boss Granny herself.

"Now I'm not going to waste your time. You're busy, I'm busy, even Billy Wayne here is busy." She smiled at Bobbi June's husband. He looked scared. She'd have to keep him on a short leash, that was for sure.

"You've lost an endowed chair, is what I hear," she continued, "and

I'm going to offer you another one to kind of replace it. I know what it costs, and I've got the money for it. But I've also got some conditions of my own."

Here the president glanced at Billy Wayne. "Dean Kilgore," he began, "I'd appreciate—"

"Let me just say to begin with," interrupted Billy Wayne, "that I am here to facilitate this, but I am in no way interested in it. That is, I am interested in it because I believe in the future of this institution. But I am not personally interested. The wife and I—you know Bobbi June, President Cager—we've had a long talk, and we've decided it's in our best interest, the best interests of our family, if I return to teaching. Effective this fall. September, that is. If you can replace me."

"I think we can manage that," said the president. "I hate to lose a good man, though."

"You boys can straighten all that out later. We were talking about endowing this chair, as I recall."

"Of course," said the president. "The college is certainly interested in your proposition."

"Well, Full Court Press is prepared to endow a chair but not the same one Dixie Mushrooms pulled out from under you."

"Not the one Booth Hazard recently occupied?"

"No," said Boss Granny, "kiss that chair good-bye. Full Court wants a brand new chair, and this one's to be made over to Bertha Michaels for as long as she wants to sit in it. Full Court will keep it going into the wild blue, and that's a promise. But it's got to be Bertha's now and until she decides to retire. Hers without question and with all the perks, same as the mushroom guy got with his chair. That's the deal, and I hope you like it, because I sure as hell do."

Had she blushed? Never mind. The president shook her hand. Then Billy Wayne's.

Chapter 42
The Last Chapter

Arden had been lying in bed, reading late, taking thoughtful leave of the author whose words for five hundred thirty-six pages had shaped her life. Now that Alice was home, in fact, lay sleeping beside her, what need had she of the soporific of criticism? Page 563 concluded,

The wedding, with which the novel of manners inevitably concludes, symbolically celebrates the mending of several crucial, socially crippling disjunctures, principally those between: 1) appearance and reality, 2) head and heart, and 3) male and female. By virtue of her marriage and the awarding of a new name (not to mention the customary acquisition of a fine country estate), the heroine of the novel of manners now takes her rightful place in society, her identity at last legitimized.

No, thought Arden. I remain largely illegal.

Letting the book slip from her hand and slide softly onto the floor, she snuggled close to her beloved Alice, who lay in peace. How grateful she felt! Here she was, this very moment, breathing in the slightly damp and aromatic hair of her Alice, the summer semester over and properly celebrated.

In this fine country estate, they all reclined, if not slept. Except, of course, for Topaz, who, with Nancy Smith from the university, was rehearsing late for Eight Days of Dance. In an hour or two he would walk through the moonlit evening, up the front steps, pausing, perhaps on the porch to choreograph a new section for the tuxedo number, and on to his room. Then they would all be asleep in this house under the stars.

But now she was definitely not.

Instead she was wide awake. The old moon streamed in her window sending waves of light across the sheet, luminous shocks of energy calling for attention, expenditure, movement of some kind. Something remained to be done. She felt it at the back of her mind. Some domestic task pleading for completion. What was it?

And then she remembered. The flag, that was it. Lowering the flag at sundown was Topaz's chore this week, and before leaving this afternoon he had asked her to do it for him.

As if sensing her restlessness, Alice stirred, then turned over. Alice, who could always sleep. Arden waited quietly, listening for her breath to fall into graceful patterns, like dolphins rolling through tranquil dark seas. At last Arden eased carefully out of bed and tiptoed down the stairs.

Outside on the front porch, she stood in her pajamas, yielding to the moist embrace of the night, the bright, nearly full moon. There was wind up there tonight. Dark clouds streaked past the luminous face, while here below everything remained still. The flag hung in the silence, as if about to speak. Then off in the woods she heard an owl call. A moment passed, and then a second owl answered. The hunters were out tonight, she knew, working the clearings in pairs, vigilant for carelessness or need.

Arden reached up to release the rope, lowered the flag into her arms, folded it carefully, musing all the while on time and work and geography and on love, that strange foreign language.

She clutched the red flag to her breast, suffused with wonder and even gratitude, asking blessings of Tonantzín, Malinche, Coatlicue, they who had brought her to this place. For somehow she was here at last, with her own love. "Alice," she said into the night, "we're home."

But why was she standing on the porch in her pajamas, when she could be upstairs in bed with Alice? She set the triangle of flag reverently on the table in the hallway, ready for tomorrow, and climbed the stairs.

At the landing she heard a child stir, murmur. She paused in Ellen's doorway, listening, breathing in her child dream, and then, drawn forth by impulse, she crossed the moon-struck floor to adjust her covers, moving on to the window, marking the forest's silhouette against the line of the sky. At the top of the world a moist circle hovered about the moon, almost like a kiss, she thought, swooning toward language.

Across the field a light burned late in Hattie's bedroom window. Hattie, who had risked and spent so much for her. They had all done that, had they not? Bertha, Boss Granny, and Bobbi June too, each in her own way. Perhaps there had always been women keeping watch like this, whispering directions and encouragement to those traversing open field or mined terrain. A legion of watchers.

And were they now all safe?

Ah, if she knew that. She looked out over the breathing gardens, at the dark leaves holding light as if for a reason.